"What are you running from?" he asked.

Kelly went hot and cold by turns as shock ripped through her. How had he known? What had she said? How had her most closely guarded secret been so obvious? When she managed to find her voice, she said, "I don't know what you mean."

"I think you do," he said quietly.

"You don't know anything about me!"

"That's true. And it's none of my business, really. But the way you opened the door this afternoon, looking like a frightened gazelle, and rented this crappy place in a town in the middle of nowhere… Sorry. I don't think you're on a vacation."

"It doesn't matter what I am."

"Maybe not." He leaned back a bit in his chair as if to give her more space. "I guess I've outstayed my welcome."

She didn't want him to go. Didn't want to rattle around alone in this house, not yet.

"Wait," she said tautly.

★ ★ ★

Dear Reader,

Many of us try to take too much responsibility for the things that happen in life. It is not as if we are fully in control of much, but who among us hasn't at one time or another castigated ourselves for what we "should have done?"

We act as best we can in a given situation, with the information we have and understand at the time. In retrospect, we might think we should have done or said something different, but at the time we didn't know what we learned later.

Given this kind of thinking, victims too often blame themselves. "I should have" is one of the saddest cries we make. "I should have known." "I should have done something else." "I should have guessed." The guilt is a heavy burden.

This kind of hindsight can cause terrific problems for us, especially if the consequences were grave. In this story, a man deals with survivor guilt, and a woman deals with guilt over being victimized by the man she once loved. This is the story of how they learn to forgive themselves and find their ultimate healing in love.

It's also a bit of a thriller. Enjoy!

Hugs,

Rachel

RACHEL LEE

Just a Cowboy

ROMANTIC
SUSPENSE

Recycling programs
for this product may
not exist in your area.

ISBN-13: 978-0-373-27733-9

JUST A COWBOY

Books by Rachel Lee

Harlequin Romantic Suspense
***The Final Mission* #1655
**Just a Cowboy #1663

Silhouette Romantic Suspense
An Officer and a Gentleman #370
 Serious Risks #394
 Defying Gravity #430
**Exile's End* #449
*Cherokee Thunder #463
**Miss Emmaline and the Archangel* #482
*Ironheart #494
*Lost Warriors #535
**Point of No Return* #566
**A Question of Justice* #613
*Nighthawk #781
**Cowboy Comes Home* #865
**Involuntary Daddy* #955
Holiday Heroes #1487
***A Soldier's Homecoming* #1519
**Protector of One #1555
***The Unexpected Hero* #1567
***The Man from Nowhere* #1595
***Her Hero in Hiding* #1611
***A Soldier's Redemption* #1635
**No Ordinary Hero #1643

Silhouette Shadows
Imminent Thunder #10
*Thunder Mountain #37

Silhouette Books
**A Conard County Reckoning*
*Conard County
The Heart's Command
 "Dream Marine"

Montana Mavericks
Cowboy Cop #12

**World's Most
Eligible Bachelors**
**The Catch of Conard County*

*Conard County
***Conard County:*
 The Next Generation

RACHEL LEE

was hooked on writing by the age of twelve, and practiced her craft as she moved from place to place all over the United States. This *New York Times* bestselling author now resides in Florida and has the joy of writing full-time.

Her bestselling Conard County series (see www.conardcounty.com) has won the hearts of readers worldwide, and it's no wonder, given her own approach to life and love. As she says, "Life is the biggest romantic adventure of all—and if you're open and aware, the most marvelous things are just waiting to be discovered." Readers can email Rachel at RachelLee@ConardCounty.com.

To Kristin T., a quiet hero.

Prologue

Kelly Scanlon Devereaux drove home late and alone. It was fast approaching midnight, the downside of having lost her job along with her marriage. She'd had to take a temporary position waiting tables, and it was beginning to look as if she'd never work again as a medical billing clerk. At least not around here.

That was the cost of divorcing a prominent plastic surgeon: No other doctor wanted to hire her under the circumstances, and so far the hospitals had had no openings.

At least she had shed Dean Devereaux. Mostly. There was still the divorce to get through in a few months, but in the meantime she had her own place and didn't have to live in constant terror that she would to make Dean mad.

Only now that she was free of that threat did she realize just how nervous and tense she had been for most of the last eight years. Now she often wondered why she had put up with it for so long.

She knew her way around Miami like the back of her hand and chose her route to avoid dangerous neighborhoods. It made her trip longer, but she didn't care. A little extra time in the car was a small price to pay for freedom.

The truth was, however, that she wouldn't feel truly free until the divorce was final. Her hands tightened on the steering wheel as the anxiety hit her again, and she took a couple of deep breaths to steady herself.

Up until today, Dean had been ugly about the whole thing. He didn't like losing, and watching him over the last few months since she'd filed for divorce had been an eye-opener. That man actually thought of her as a possession.

He'd fought the court's decision to give her separate maintenance and had lost. Her attorney had had to hire forensic accountants to find his assets. And she had been mad enough about the way he had treated her, especially over the last year of their marriage when he had started to hit her, that she had wanted to gouge him.

Cripes, he'd even told her she wasn't going to live long enough to see a settlement. Ugly, ugly.

But today, just today, her lawyer had called to tell her that Dean had agreed to the settlement, that he had signed the papers.

She was still reeling from that. Her attorney assured her that Dean had changed his mind in order to avoid the publicity of a messy trial, in which his own wife would accuse him of physical abuse, and maybe the lawyer was right. It could hardly help the practice of a man who spent his life making beautiful, wealthy women more beautiful to have it known that he was a wife beater.

So maybe the end was in sight. Her lawyer said Dean couldn't change his mind now, that the papers his attorney had sent were almost as good as the court's seal on the settlement.

But she realized, now that she had won, that she didn't care much about the money. She cared most about the painful places the whole mess had left, and worse, the realization that she hadn't been strong enough to stand up to the man all those years. That she had taken it and taken it, and blamed herself for not being good enough.

That she had been drawn in by charm, flattery and all the oiliness of a snake.

Ugh. She'd give all that money back if she could just erase the last eight years from her life.

She pulled into her parking garage at last and into her numbered slot. Like many high-rises in Miami, this one had been built so that the parking garage was beneath the apartments, at ground level, putting the living units well above the reach of a storm surge in hurricane season. She often thought that if they hadn't had to put the building on stilts, there would have been no garage at all. This address wasn't exactly A-list.

But it was good enough, she reminded herself. She sat for a few minutes in her car, enjoying the quiet after work, the sense that soon it would all be over and Dean would be firmly in her past. The sense that she was about to reach a point where she could finally shed the emotional bruises and stop living in fear.

God, it was going to be a relief. Increasingly, she dreamed of leaving Miami permanently. The more miles she could put between her and Dean, the better. She didn't want to hear his name ever again, even by accident. Heck, she wouldn't turn on her TV because she might run across one of the commercials for his practice.

Nor did she have any ties holding her here. All the friends she thought she had made during her marriage had turned their backs on her. Maybe she made them uncomfortable in some way, because she suspected many of their marriages were like hers. Women who had married wealthy men who had turned out to think of them as possessions.

"You pay for that money," she whispered, facing up to her mistake yet again. Even when you honestly believed you loved the guy, you wound up paying for the luxury...sometimes with your body, sometimes with your soul. She'd paid with a little of both.

At last she sighed and climbed out of her car, thinking of crawling into bed and just *forgetting* everything for a few hours. All the stress, all the worry, even some of the self-loathing she still felt.

Oh, she'd been stupid and naive to begin with, but later, as the emotional abuse mounted, her excuses had grown thinner. She didn't like herself for that.

She was walking toward the elevator when a voice called out, "Mrs. Devereaux?"

At once a shudder of distaste ran down her spine. Thinking it was one of the security guards, she turned. "I prefer Ms. Scanlon now."

The man stood only a foot away, dressed Miami casual, smiling. "I thought I recognized you. My sister-in-law goes to see your husband. Anyway, you dropped something when you got out of the car."

She looked at the hand he held out, trying to see what it was, caught a blur from the corner of her eye, then the world exploded in blackness and stars as her head seemed to split open.

I'm going to die.

And then she thought nothing at all.

Chapter 1

Coming home from roundup at a local ranch in Conard County, Hank Jackson expected to unload his gear, step into the cool quiet of his house, and maybe have a shot of bourbon to ease the pain he lived with constantly.

It seemed that no matter how well the docs put smashed bones back together, the bones always remembered the insult. Then they couldn't make up their minds if they hated activity or inactivity more.

Regardless, more than a week on the range of riding, camping, roping and herding had left his body feeling a little older than its thirty-four years, and he was looking for a hot bath and a shot, not necessarily in that order.

Except as he was tugging his saddle out of the back of his pickup, he noticed the house next door. He owned that place, too, a decision made on the spur of the moment because he preferred being busy to having too much time on his hands to think, and that house would keep an entire crew of repairmen busy for quite a while.

But since he had left nine days ago, things had changed, signaled by curtains in the windows.

Crap. He froze, saddle still resting on the truck bed, and looked again. He should never have let Ben Patterson persuade him to list the place for rent a few weeks ago. There was still a ton of work that needed to be done, as he'd told Ben. Then he'd allowed himself to be talked into listing it because it would propel him to get the work done faster.

Hell.

He'd never expected that anyone would take it in that condition, not even at the ridiculously low rent.

Sighing, he shifted his weight onto the hip that hurt marginally less and tried to decide if he could ignore his new tenant until tomorrow. Or was he honor-bound to get the heck over there right now and tell him all about the things that weren't working right and a few things that might not be safe?

Ben might not have remembered all the details. And what if there was a family in there?

Cussing under his breath, he left his saddle and headed next door, leaving his own grassy yard behind for the weedy patch of dirt that belonged to the other house. Yet another thing he'd been planning to take care of this week or next.

Climbing the two steps to the small, covered porch elicited another cuss word that only he could hear. The doorbell didn't work, so he rapped sharply on the front door, a solid oak door in dire need of painting. Oh, hell, why kid himself? It needed a blow-torch first, and looking at it he was quite certain some of the underlying layers of paint were lead-based. He'd better not find any kids living here, because, if he did, Ben would get more than a few choice words.

His first knock went unanswered. He rapped again, more

loudly, saw one of the new curtains twitch, and finally the front door opened a crack.

He found himself looking into one blue eye through that crack.

"Yes?" said a quiet, tense voice.

"Hank Jackson," he said. "I'm your landlord."

"Oh." Then, "Oh! The agent mentioned you."

And the door didn't open even a hair wider. "Lady, I don't know if Ben bothered to tell you, but there are some things about this house that aren't safe."

"I know that."

"But do you know them all? Just tell me you don't have any kids."

"No. No kids."

This wasn't getting them very far. Part of him just wanted to turn around, walk away, find that hot bath and that shot of bourbon. But in good conscience he couldn't do that without at least making an attempt.

"I need to show you the things that are wrong. I need to tell you the work I'm going to be doing in the next week or so. Ben *did* tell you I'd be working on the place?"

"It can wait. I'll only be here a short while."

"Some of it can't wait." Damn, she was bringing out his stubborn streak. "Look, I don't bite, but I may have to break your rental agreement if we don't come to some kind of terms about the things I need to do here."

The door opened a little wider and he was astonished to see the kind of blond, blue-eyed beauty that should be in the movies. And she looked nervous. Why the heck should she look nervous? Nobody in Conard County looked nervous about someone knocking on the door.

He almost sighed. Instead, he fought for some courtesy. "It's important," he said. "I didn't expect the place to get rented in its current condition, and I'm not sure Ben gave you all the warnings."

At last she nodded, opened the door all the way, and let him step in. He smothered a wince as his hip reminded him that not all was well south of the border, especially after a week in the saddle.

"The place is good enough for me," she said tentatively. "I'll only be here a short time."

"Yeah, but I'd like you to leave on your feet, not on a stretcher."

At that he was relieved to see the faintest of smiles lift the corners of her perfect mouth. Beauty came in all varieties, but this woman had the kind that usually implied heaps of plastic surgery. Exactly the kind that didn't appeal a whole lot to him. Usually.

"The place isn't exactly a death trap," he said, forcing himself to pay attention to business and not to another area south of the border that was choosing a bad time to sit up and take notice. "But there's some rotten flooring I need to warn you about, and a couple of iffy electrical circuits. And the stove doesn't work right, but I have a replacement coming soon."

"Okay."

He held out his hand. "Hank Jackson."

"Kelly Scanlon." Her handshake was firm. Okay, so she hadn't come by that perfect figure by unnatural means. She must work out.

"Nice to meet you," he managed to say as if he meant it, although he was thinking of at least a half-dozen ways he'd like to give Ben a hard time.

"If the house is so bad, why are you renting it?" she asked.

"It wasn't my intention. Ben's been after me to list it with him. I thought I made it clear he wasn't to rent it until I'd finished the most important work."

Her smile widened a shade. "I guess he doesn't listen well?"

"Apparently not. Either that, or he's even more desperate than I thought. Even with the semiconductor plant that moved in a couple of years ago, I think beggars around here make more than real estate agents. Did he even show you the fuse box?"

"No."

"Hell." He sighed, then limped past her through the small living room to the kitchen. Like many kitchens of its era, it had more room than convenience. Space enough for a big table, but few cabinets, an old freestanding sink, and just an itty-bitty patch of counter. The stove stood all by itself near one wall, the refrigerator a few feet away.

"Someday," he remarked, "this is going to be a nice kitchen. But right now..." He shook his head. "Most of it looks like an afterthought."

"I don't need much."

"Maybe not," he allowed. "One person can get by." He walked over to the mudroom door and stepped out into the unheated, glassed-in area. "Here's the fuse box."

He opened the metal casing. "There are three circuits here that I removed the fuses from. Resist any temptation to put a fuse in them until I get an electrician out here. If you get desperate to use these circuits, I have extension cords I can lend you so you can plug into safe sockets."

"Okay, I can do that."

He glanced over and found her standing right at his shoulder. And damn, she smelled good, too. Faintly like roses and honey. Or maybe after a week of smelling horses and cattle, anything else would smell like ambrosia.

He tore his gaze from her—for some reason his eyes kept

wanting to stare—and pointed to the floor to the right side of the back door. "Over there the joists are rotting underneath. You can go out the door safely, but I'd advise against stepping over there. I can't guarantee it will hold you."

"Okay." She sounded agreeable enough.

He looked at her again. "Did Ben tell you this?"

She bit her lip, then gave a tiny shake of her head.

He sighed. "Oh, I am going to have some words with him. All right, the windows out here are slated to be replaced. I have the new ones in my garage, but I haven't gotten to it yet. You'll notice the windows in the rest of the house are all new, but I still need to do some caulking and leveling, okay? So you'll have me outside from time to time banging around."

"Okay."

That seemed to be her only word. He led the way back through the kitchen to the rear of the house, where there were two bedrooms. One was completely empty, the other held an old bedstead. He just hadn't gotten around to removing it, or some of the other furniture the last owners had left behind. Not much, but a minimum for someone who had none.

But when he looked at the bedstead and mattress, he winced, and this time it wasn't from physical pain. "Are you going to sleep on that?" he asked.

"It's there."

"Ah, crap, lady, that thing is…"

"A bed," she said firmly. "I can get a mattress pad to cover the worst of it. At least it's not the floor."

This time when he looked at her he saw past the initial impression of too beautiful to something that showed more depth and determination. Eyes that appeared older than her appearance would indicate. There was a story there, he thought. He wasn't sure he wanted to know it, either. She'd made it clear she was a transient, and he knew the kinds of stories that came with eyes like that.

"The stuff that's here," he said by way of explanation, "was left by the previous owners. I just haven't gotten around to getting rid of it. If you want it out of here…"

She interrupted. "No, really. I can use the stuff that's here. I don't need or want to replace it."

"Your choice," he said after a moment. "Watch it in the empty bedroom, though. More rotten floors. I got rid of the termites, but I just haven't had time yet to replace all the wood."

"Not a problem."

He scanned the rooms again, and never had the place looked shabbier. It was an old house to begin with, and the last owners hadn't invested much, if anything, in keeping it up. They'd been getting on in years, and probably hadn't even noticed most of the deterioration. The walls everywhere were hideous, covered in dying wallpaper, water spots and paint that had probably been sagging on the walls since the Second World War. The floors…well, where they weren't bare, worn wood, they were covered by old, cheap linoleum that had been tacked down in places where it had ripped.

"I was so sure nobody would rent this place in this condition."

She surprised him with a quiet laugh. "Amazing things happen."

He looked at her again and felt himself smiling in response. "That they do."

"Sorry I can't offer you coffee or anything, but I just rented the place this morning and I haven't been out to get supplies, or even any dishes or a coffeemaker. I figured I could do that tomorrow."

"This morning? Just this morning?" That gave him pause. "You have a car, right?"

She shook her head.

"Well, hell," he said. "That's not gonna work. You can't

carry much on foot—the store's on the other side of town. What do you need?"

She shrugged a shoulder. "That depends on how comfortable I want to be."

"Short term, right?"

"Two months at most."

He nodded. "Okay. I've got some stuff at my place you can use. Coffeemaker, pots and pans, some spare dishes and things. No reason you should buy that stuff for just a couple of months."

Her mouth opened a little in surprise. "Are you sure you can spare it?"

"Hell, yeah. That house belonged to my parents. When I moved back here, I came with a lot of stuff from my place in Denver. I wanted my own things, and I just moved a lot of theirs to the side." Feeling a little awkward, he admitted, "I just wasn't ready to get rid of it, you know?"

She nodded. "But now? Are you comfortable with somebody else using it?"

"Sure. I'm not lending you the heirloom china, though."

She laughed again, and this time it was an easier sound. That was good. If he was going to have to deal with a tenant as closely as he'd need to deal with this one, what with all the work this place needed quickly, it was far better to deal with one who wasn't uptight about everything.

And the rest of it? Well that was just being neighborly.

"Come on," he said. "I'll get you some minimum stuff to get through the night, and we can discuss what else you need in the morning."

"But," she said, "Ben said you were out working at one of the ranches. You must be tired."

"I am. But if I stop moving, I'll freeze up. So let's just get you a coffeepot, some dishes. Like I said, just enough for tonight. We can deal with anything else in the morning."

Then he turned and limped his way to the front door, aware of her light step following him.

Kelly followed him, noticing the limp, but even more noticing his lean, rangy build, a build that, encased in jeans and a plaid Western shirt, suggested a lot of hard muscle beneath. His face had a chiseled appearance, a few lines that seemed awfully deep for a guy who didn't look like he was much older than she was, and the sun had bronzed him. His hair was dark and a little wavy, and just a bit too long.

He was the kind of guy a lot of women in her previous life would have noticed, partly because he had a great build, but partly because he was so different from what they were accustomed to. A rednecked cowboy, evidently, and a far cry from the guys she had known who got their muscles in gyms and their tans on the beach or in salons.

She had to admit that she liked it. Life with her soon-to-be-ex husband had revolved around his practice and the hours he spent with a personal trainer. Not to mention the careful artifice of sun-streaked hair from a bottle.

Once that had seemed normal to her, but now she loathed the plasticity of it. Which was really kind of a funny thought, since Dean had been a plastic surgeon. She swallowed a giggle, surprised that she even wanted to laugh.

"So," said Hank Jackson, the limping cowboy who had just barged into her life, "how the heck did you get curtains up so fast?"

"It was the first thing I did this morning," she answered truthfully. "I walked into town and bought them. The rods were still good."

"Yeah, I hadn't pulled them down, either." He paused at the steps to his porch and looked at her. "I've always heard that the first thing women do in a new place is put up curtains. Never believed it before."

"Well, you can believe it now." Nor did she have any intention of telling him why those curtains were so important to her.

"I guess not all stereotypes are stereotypes," he remarked. He tugged a key out of his pocket and unlocked the front door.

The house smelled a tiny bit stale, having been closed up for a while, but it wasn't a bad stale. Just faint hints that meals had been cooked here, that someone had lived here and been away.

It had a similar layout to her place, although it was a bit bigger. And the signs of a woman's presence still dominated. She guessed that he hadn't been able to part with a lot, including dotted Swiss curtains with ruffles, cheerful rag rugs and picture frames holding bunches of dried flowers.

He led her down the hallway, much longer than the tiny one in her place, to a large kitchen. Unlike hers, this one had been modernized with new cabinets, a dishwasher, a stainless-steel stove and a matching refrigerator.

"Let me get some boxes," he said, and disappeared through a door.

She waited, looking around, and felt her throat tighten unwillingly. This place practically shouted "home," unlike the mansion she'd left behind. Sometimes she wondered how she could have been so stupid and blind.

Hank returned a couple of minutes later with a box under each arm. "I think a lot of what you need is already here."

He set them on the table and she moved closer to look as he opened them.

"Ah, I do have a memory," he said wryly as he revealed a drip coffeemaker, some dishes and flatware.

"This is terribly kind of you," she said honestly. "I'd have managed."

"I'm sure you would have, but when you have a neighbor,

it's not always necessary. And if you're only going to stay a few weeks, it just makes sense to lend you my extras."

"Thank you."

He smiled, an expression that lit up his face. "Let's get this stuff over there, and come back for some more. You cook a lot?"

"Not really." Not anymore. Life with Dean had meant dining out nearly every night, and when dining at home there'd been guests and a cook. Funny how that all looked to her in retrospect. But she didn't want to think about that now.

It felt odd, after weeks on the run, to be trusting someone again, even if the trust only went as far as to let her new landlord lend her some things. Her nerve endings had been crawling for so long that she wasn't sure they were capable of stopping.

But she was sure she had found the most out-of-the-way place on the planet, short of Antarctica, and something about this little town nestled in the middle of nowhere had suggested that she might be able to safely pause and catch her breath. She could be wrong, and she promised herself that at the first suggestion of danger, she would bolt like a rabbit.

One thing for sure: She needed a little time free from being constantly on the move. Even if it was only a few days or a week.

"I can't thank you enough," she repeated as he unloaded the boxes onto her kitchen table and suggested that they go back for more.

"No need," he insisted reassuringly. "I'm not using these things and you need them for a few weeks. It's really not a big deal."

It was to her, but Kelly didn't say so. Up to now, the only help she had received from anyone had been a few drivers who had given her a lift when she decided she needed to get away from buses for a while.

By the time Hank finished taking care of her, she had sheets, towels, pots, pans and some kitchen utensils.

"If you need anything else," he said as he unloaded the last ones, "just give me a shout. I'm sure I've forgotten something, and I have plenty in storage."

"You're very kind."

He shook his head, looking almost wry. "That's what neighbors do. Although I have to admit, it's not helping me work on my future as a crusty curmudgeon."

That surprised a laugh out of her, and she liked the way his gray eyes seemed to dance in response. "Really? You want to be a curmudgeon?"

"Of course. I still have a long way to go. Haven't been able to bring myself to yell at the kids to stay out of my yard… although I may get there when I lay the sod out front next week."

"Why are you sodding?"

He leaned back against the counter and folded his arms. "Because if I seed, it'll rain and wash it all away…and I really don't fancy the idea of trying to scoop up all the seed in a spoon and sprinkle it around again." He paused while she laughed quietly again at the image. "Or, if it doesn't rain, the neighborhood kids I still can't bring myself to yell at will be all over it, killing the shoots before they have a chance."

"And that would make you yell?"

He sighed and ran his fingers through shaggy, dark hair. "No, it probably wouldn't. So I'll just avoid all the problems and lay sod. It should stand up to just about anything except a baseball game. Now what about food? You must need to get some. Just let me get that saddle out of my truck and we'll go."

"I've already imposed enough," she said firmly.

"I need to go to the store anyway. I've been out on the range for about nine days. I'm afraid to open my refrigerator. Grab whatever you need while I get my gear stowed, then we'll go."

She followed him to the door, and once again noticed the way he limped as he walked back to his place. She wondered what had happened to him.

Then she told herself it didn't matter. Two months, max, and she'd be out of here. Sooner if necessary.

So it really didn't matter at all.

Chapter 2

It felt odd to have someone to talk to again. Someone she needed to talk to or seem discourteous. For the last several months she'd been on the run, exchanging as few words as possible with strangers, lying about her name and even keeping her communications with her lawyer as brief as possible.

She'd been living off cash from her mother's estate, using pay phones and basically doing what she had heard was called "living off the grid." All because she was getting a divorce. All because Dean had gotten furious with her and told her she wouldn't live to collect a settlement, and then a few weeks later some guy had attacked her and tried to drown her.

Even the cops didn't believe that Dean had been behind that. Even the cops. But she knew Dean in a way the cops didn't. She had seen his ruthless side, and when it came to money, few were as ruthless as Dean.

She sighed, and the man in the seat beside her in the old pickup looked her way. "Something wrong?" he asked.

"No. Just feeling tired I guess." Being tired covered a multitude of sins and failings, at least with people you didn't know.

"Yeah, I'm a little worn out, too," Hank said. "But it won't take long to get you some food. Enough for a day or two. We can always come back another time."

She was still trying to absorb this helpfulness. She wasn't used to it—not anymore. In the world she had just left, you paid for help or you didn't get a whole lot of it. Heck, even her few girlfriends thought she was nuts to leave Dean. But they didn't know.

And in retrospect, she wasn't sure their lives were all that much better. Did a woman have to sell her soul to live in comfort, belong to a country club and move in the right circles? Maybe so.

The main thing she wondered about was how she could ever have thought those things were important.

She cleared her throat, trying to think of something casual to say. Had she even lost her capacity for pointless conversation? After so many years of it, she would have thought it was engraved in her brain.

Except the man sitting beside her didn't seem like the type who would appreciate the inanities that had made up so much of her social life over the last eight years.

"Why," she managed finally, "do you think Ben rented me the house if you didn't want him to yet?"

"I plan to ask him. But, as I said, the real estate business isn't exactly booming around here. We got that new semiconductor plant five years ago, and for a while it looked like we were going to become the kind of town people didn't keep leaving."

"But?"

"But they laid off about two hundred people last fall. Doesn't seem like much until you see all the empty apartments and houses, and see the way local businesses are struggling again. Boom and bust. Story of this town from the beginning."

That at least gave her an opening. "How's that?"

"Well, first they found gold up there on Thunder Mountain." He pointed to the looming mountain range. "That played out in about ten years. Then came a kind of heyday for ranching. Lots of cattle, lots of wide-open space, enough water, believe it or not. Those were the days of the big spreads, and folks in town were just here to supply ranchers' needs basically."

Kelly nodded. "And then?"

"Raising cattle got out-of-sight expensive, people wouldn't pay the price, beef got shipped in from Argentina and things turned kind of black around here for a while."

"And now?"

"The ranches are mostly smaller, some folks still make money off beef, some are raising sheep, others horses. Then we got the semiconductor plant, and for a while there were plenty of jobs for young folks, and people with special skills moved here and we kinda grew again."

"But now it's bad."

"Now it's rough. The way it is everywhere, it seems. We thought we might get a ski resort up in the mountains, but that folded up pretty fast. We aren't close enough to a major population center to have a load of people drive out here, and while we've got an airport, it would need a major expansion to bring in enough skiers. I guess you could say we didn't have the kind of money necessary to make ourselves attractive."

She nodded, absorbing what he was saying. "So everyone here is hurting?"

"Not really. We've just gone back to our belt-tightening ways. We get by on what we have—it's not like we're going to dry up and blow away. I guess it's just kind of an interest of mine, to think about how this town starts to grow and then shrinks back again. It's almost like breathing." He chuckled quietly.

"That's a different way of looking at it. But I agree. This place doesn't look like it's going away. The first thing that struck me about it is that it seems to have always been here."

"Not quite always, but well over a century now. Was that what made you decide to stay here? Because we sure don't seem to have a lot to offer most people, at least ones who didn't grow up here."

She hesitated, trying to find a way to put into words what had made her pause here in her journey, without revealing too much. "I guess…well, the place just feels…" She hesitated again and then gave a nervous laugh. "It's sounds stupid, but when I got here what I felt was reliability. You know, like you could always count on this town."

He turned into the grocery store lot and parked before he spoke. "Maybe that's a good word for it," he said finally. "Reliability. There's a lot of that around here."

Then he paused. "Well, except for Ben Patterson. I told him that place isn't safe yet."

"Maybe he just figured it wouldn't be a problem because I wanted it for such a short time." She bit her lower lip. "Look, if you want me to move, I will. But it's just so hard to find a place that doesn't want to tie me into a long-term lease."

His gray eyes focused on her with an intensity that made her nervous. As if he were seeing things she was sure she hadn't revealed. Then came the question she had hoped to avoid but had known, deep in her heart, she wouldn't be able to.

"Why do you want to keep moving?"

It was, however, a question for which she'd already thought

up the answer, weeks ago, just in case. "I'm traveling around the country is all. I finally reached a point where I could do it, and so I just decided to do it."

To her it almost seemed as if he frowned, though she couldn't point to a single thing in his face that changed. After a moment he shrugged. "Some folks have wanderlust, I guess."

"It's not exactly wanderlust. It's just that…well, I might never get the chance to do this again. It seemed like a good time." She hoped she never *had* to do this again, but that was a different story, one she wasn't prepared to discuss with a stranger. Nor was she about to tell anyone that the only hope she cherished was that she had covered her tracks well enough. Sometimes she feared she hadn't.

He seemed satisfied, though, and climbed out of the truck. She came around from her side and watched him stretch a little, as if things ached.

"Being a cowboy is hard work?" she asked, deciding to let him explain it any way he wanted.

"It can be, but damn, it's great. Wide-open spaces, sleeping under starry skies, cooking over campfires. I like it."

"Do you do it all the time?"

He twisted his back a little then shook his arms. "When there's work. When I can."

The answers sounded short, so she let it go. She was hardly likely to press him to go places when there were plenty of them she didn't want to go herself.

They shopped separately and met back at the truck. She had only bought enough for a couple of days, but he seemed to have bought considerably more. She helped him load bags into the back of the pickup, and then they headed back to the house.

"You need anything else," he said after he helped her carry

her stuff inside, "you let me know. And don't go scratching at the walls. God knows what's under that paper."

At that she laughed again, suddenly feeling better than she had in a couple of months.

"What's so funny?" he asked.

"The idea of what could be under that paper. You've been talking about this house like it's a ticking time bomb."

A smile lit his face. "Maybe it is. Admittedly, the last folks who lived there made it to their nineties, so for all I know it's the Fountain of Youth."

She had a nice laugh, he thought as he headed back to his place, focused on finally getting that hot bath and that shot of bourbon. Or maybe he'd go over to Mahoney's tonight instead and shoot the breeze with some of the regulars.

Of course, the problem with that was, inevitably, someone would get drunk enough to ask him about his firefighting days. And no matter how often he made it clear that he was just a cowboy now, there was always some jerk who didn't get the memo, at least once he was a little drunk.

Most folks hereabouts *had* gotten the memo and didn't bring up the subject anymore. And that was just the way he wanted it.

He shook the thought away. One of the best things he could say about Conard County was that folks tended to drop things you wanted dropped. At least to your face. They might gossip like mad among themselves, but they wouldn't keep bringing it up to you.

And he didn't want to think about that right now. In fact, he'd have been happy not to think about it at all.

Settling into the tub full of hot water, he released a sigh and turned his thoughts in other directions. Like Ben Patterson, with whom he was going to have more than a couple of words soon. And his new tenant.

Kelly Scanlon. He liked the name but her very presence raised a lot of questions. He had honestly believed that Ben wouldn't be able to rent that place at any price, warnings attached or not. It was barely livable, and just knowing there was someone over there now made him feel like a grade-A slumlord.

He'd agreed to list it because Ben had been full of talk about how people never moved overnight, that listing it would be good because the place was going to be ready in a couple of months.

That had made sense to Hank. Let people know the property would be available down the road. He'd agreed when Ben had said most people planned their moves in advance anyway.

So, yeah, it had made sense. Certainly, he'd never expected a total stranger to turn up out of the blue wanting the place right now, in its current condition, for only a couple of months. Weird.

And that weirdness made him think about Kelly Scanlon. Her nervousness when she'd opened the door. That haunted look in her eyes. That kind of woman seldom went begging for anything. Men would trip all over themselves to look after her.

Or maybe not.

He sighed, let his head fall back against the rolled-up towel he'd strategically placed on the edge of the tub, and closed his eyes.

Something was not right over there. The thought drifted through his mind, and since he hadn't poured that shot of bourbon, he knew he couldn't blame it on anything except instinct.

His instincts were sharp, honed by years of fighting fires. He never ignored them, unless someone else's life was on the line.

And his instincts were trying to tell him that something was very wrong. Well, sheesh, it wouldn't take a genius to figure that out, he supposed.

Woman comes out of nowhere—gorgeous woman, making it even odder—to rent a house just this side of condemned for a couple of months in a town in the middle of nowhere. Sure, that sounded perfectly normal.

He sighed again, sinking a little lower into the soothing water and raised his knees one at a time to loosen the kinks.

Okay, it was strange. It was also not his problem, beyond making sure she didn't get hurt because of that house. Hell, was he ever going to roast Ben over some hot coals. How many times had he told the agent that the house was not completely safe?

It wasn't likely to collapse on Kelly's head, but things could happen. The termite damage, some of the dubious wiring, even a stove with a pilot light…

Dammit. He sat up suddenly, ignoring a spear of pain. He hadn't gotten to that part. And he'd bet dollars to doughnuts that Ben had been real friendly and had turned the propane on for her. Not that it was all that bad. The thing had an automatic shutoff when the pilot went out, which was the only reason he hadn't just ripped it out of the house already.

But still.

Oh, what the… He didn't bother to complete the thought. The water was cooling down anyway, and he could take another bath if he needed to soak some more.

Rising, water sluicing off him in waves, he stepped out onto the mat and reached for a towel.

Five minutes later he was limping next door, water droplets still clinging to the ends of his hair.

Kelly didn't want to answer the knock. It was getting dark outside, although the evenings were a lot longer here than she was used to. She didn't even want to twitch a curtain back to look. She was well aware that all her attempts to evade a possible tracker might not have worked. Aware of all the times she'd had to present ID, then hit the road again the very next morning, following a crazy-quilt pattern around the country. What if her path hadn't been random enough?

Even as she hovered in hesitation in the kitchen, she told herself that she was overreacting. No one knew where she was. She had tried to make darn sure of that. So the only person who could be at her door was her too-attractive landlord, the real estate agent who shouldn't have rented to her or a kid selling something, and it was the wrong time of year for cookies.

The knock came again, more insistent this time, and finally she squared her shoulders and went to answer it.

Twilight bathed the world outside, the long endless twilight of the northern latitudes. The sun had gone down behind the mountains early, but that didn't make the world completely darken. She had plenty of light by which to see Hank.

"I'm a fireman," he said without preamble. "Well, I was."

"Oh." How was she supposed to respond to that?

"I'm just a cowboy these days," he said rather insistently, "but that doesn't mean I've forgotten everything."

"Of course not."

"I've got to tell you about the pilot light on the stove."

Feeling confused, but strangely relieved to see him, she stepped back and waved him inside. For some reason she'd felt safer in cheap motel rooms than she felt in this house, something that surprised her. Maybe she'd found so much security in moving that she couldn't feel it any longer when she held still. Or maybe there was a reason for the uneasiness that wouldn't leave her alone. Maybe she needed to heed it until she could figure out where it was coming from.

"I just made some coffee," she offered hesitantly.

"This won't take but a minute."

For some reason, as soon as they were in the kitchen, she pulled a couple of the mugs he'd leant her out of the cupboard anyway. "Black?" she asked.

"Yeah. Please."

At least he hadn't refused again. For the first time in ages she just didn't want to be alone.

"Okay," he said, lifting the stovetop to reveal the unadorned burners and gas lines. "The pilot won't stay lit. I don't know why, I don't especially care because this thing is going. In fact, it's going tomorrow and I'm putting in the new stove since someone's living here."

"I'm sure I can manage. You don't have to do that on my account."

His gray eyes pierced her. "Yes. I do. Gas is nothing to fool with."

"No," she agreed. He seemed to want her to come over, so she left the mugs on the table and went to stand beside him.

"This is an older model, obviously. It has separate pilot lights for the stovetop and the oven. I'm going to show you how to light them both. The stove also has an automatic shutoff if the pilot goes out when the burners are turned off. They built that safety feature in years ago."

"Okay. Then there's nothing to worry about."

He shook his head. "Not exactly. I haven't been in a rush to pull it out because no one was living here and I checked the automatic shutoffs. They seem to work properly. So no gas leaks when the stove is off, even if someone turned the propane back on. I'll bet Ben turned it on for you."

"I don't know, honestly. I didn't even think to ask about it."

Stranger and stranger, he thought. She'd moved in here without even asking how to get gas for the stove?

Opening the drawer beside the stove, he pulled out a box of wooden matches and struck one. When he turned on a burner, it lit immediately. "Yeah, he turned it on for you."

"Okay."

He glanced at her and realized that she was looking puzzled, as if he was making a huge case out of nothing. But it wasn't nothing. He turned off the burner, and after about a minute, the pilot light went out. "And there's the problem."

"I see that."

"As I said, I checked and the safety shutoffs are working, so you don't need to worry about the pilots going out. But I don't know what might happen if you have a burner turned on and it goes out. I haven't cooked on this dang thing—never intended to. So I guess, what I'm saying is, don't leave it unattended while you cook until I get the new stove in here."

"I can do that," she said with certainty. "I wasn't planning on cooking anything tonight anyway, and if I do in the morning, I'll watch it."

"Thank you." He lowered the stove lid and opened the oven. "This is the pilot for the oven, but I'd really prefer you leave this one alone. This worries me because it pours out a lot of gas fast, and if the flame goes out, you won't necessarily notice and…well, you don't need me to draw you a map."

"No, I get it. But you don't have to rush to get a new stove on my account. I can manage."

He shook his head. "Ben rented this place to you. I'm responsible for your safety. That's the beginning and end of it."

"Thank you. I'll be careful."

She went quickly to get the coffee, afraid he might just stride out, and poured two mugs. He didn't hesitate, much to her relief, but took one of the chairs at the chipped dinette and reached for a mug.

She replaced the pot before joining him, and wondered

at her sudden need for companionship. Maybe it was just the strangeness of being in a house again. She hadn't really thought about that when she'd decided to rent the place for a while, but she was thinking about it now. Unlike the motel rooms she had inhabited, this place had more windows and more doors. She kept thinking about that now as darkness approached.

"So you're a firefighter?" she asked tentatively, thinking that would be a safe place to go.

Apparently not. It was almost as if his face shuttered, growing suddenly hard. Then he visibly relaxed. "Not anymore. I'm just a cowboy."

"That seems like a big career change."

"Not really. I worked as a cowpoke from the time I was twelve until I went off to the academy. Summers and vacations."

She pulled up her knee, rested her chin on it, and wrapped her arms around her leg. "I can't imagine. I've had a very different sort of life. Being a cowboy sounds exotic to me."

At that, some of the hardness slipped from his face and he smiled faintly. "It's dirty, hard, smelly work for the most part. But I've always enjoyed it. I'd do it more often if there was more work available."

"Is it like the movies?"

"In what way? We're outdoors most of the time, we pretty much work sunup to sundown. If we're working with the herds, we sleep with them. If we're working the fences, sometimes we have the shelter of a line shack if we want it. If it's romantic at all, it's the part where we sleep under the stars and sit around the campfire at night telling godawful stories. But the coffee is terrible, the food is pretty rugged and the nights can sometimes seem miserably cold."

"I've only been camping a couple of times. I liked it." She

tried a tentative smile, glad to see he'd relaxed from whatever had made him so tense.

"So what do you do?" he asked.

"I'm…I was in charge of billing for a large medical practice. I moved up to office manager, too, a couple of years ago."

"That sounds complicated. Did you like it?"

"Mostly." She closed her eyes a bit, thinking back, trying to leave Dean out of the equation. It wasn't easy. Her marriage to him had colored everything.

"Better question," he said. "Would you like to do it again?"

"Maybe." She let out a sigh and shook her head a little as she reached for her coffee. "That depends, I guess."

"With what you feel like when you're done traveling?"

"Pretty much." That seemed as safe a way to put it as any. "I have time." Two months, anyway. If she could make it that long. Once again, she assured herself she had covered her tracks. And once again some little corner at the back of her mind wasn't so sure about that. Dang it, why couldn't she put her finger on what worried her? Other than the fact that she hadn't felt safe since that man tried to drown her in a canal.

Then he dropped the boulder that left her rattled to her very core. "What are you running from?" he asked.

She went hot and cold by turns as shock ripped through her. How had he known? What had she said? Had her most closely guarded secret been so obvious? When she managed to find her voice, she said, "I don't know what you mean."

"I think you do," he said quietly.

"You don't know anything about me!"

"That's true. And it's none of my business, really."

"No, it isn't."

"But the way you opened the door this afternoon, looking like a frightened gazelle, and renting this crappy place in a town in the middle of nowhere… Sorry. I don't think you're on a vacation."

"It doesn't matter what I am."

"Maybe not." He leaned back a bit in his chair, as if to give her more space. "I guess I've overstayed my welcome. I'll be back as early as I can with the stove tomorrow, and after I get it in, I'll probably work on the windows."

He started to push back from the table, but she instantly felt bad. For the way she had just shut him out, for the rudeness she'd just displayed when he'd gone out of his way to be kind to her. But there was a bit of selfishness, too, because she didn't want him to go. Didn't want to rattle around alone in this house—not yet.

"Wait," she said tautly.

He paused, the chair only an inch farther from the table than when he'd started to shove back.

"I'm sorry. I'm being rude."

"Your business is your business."

"I know but…you've been so kind, and you're right—this is all crazy. And you're probably wondering if I'm a criminal on the lam…."

He startled her by laughing. "By God," he said, "that thought never entered my mind." Still smiling, he cocked a brow at her. "Now that could be exciting."

With all that had happened, with all she'd had to give up, she still had her sense of humor. A little giggle escaped her. "Are you that bored?"

"I don't bore easily. But I have to admit, renting a house to a fleeing felon might be one of the most interesting things I've ever done. Not the kind of thing that happens every day."

"No, it's not," she admitted, the smile still tugging at the corners of her mouth. "Sorry, I'm not running from the law."

"No surprise there."

She hesitated, then bit her lip a moment. Finally, she said, "I'll tell you, but please don't tell anyone else."

"Gossip is far from my favorite thing. And you don't have to tell me. I was just getting ready to tell you that I'm right next door if you need anything. Since you're not a felon, I won't even get in trouble for providing it. That's very dull, you know."

She liked the sparkle of humor in his eyes, liked it much better than the closed-off look she'd seen there before. Better than the man who had folded up his emotional tent because he'd just been told to mind his own business.

"Well, the truth is duller," she admitted. She could tell him part of her story, she decided. Just part. And for some idiotic reason, it seemed to want to burst out of her for the first time since she'd tried to tell the police and her lawyer. As if she'd been sitting on a powder keg of feelings for way too long and needed just one person to listen. Just one. Even her lawyer didn't quite believe her. And Hank might not, either. But the words still wanted to spill, as if she needed to vent them, regardless of the response.

"I'm getting divorced," she said.

Hank hesitated, then leaned forward, placing his elbows on the table. "I'm sorry."

"I'm not. I don't know how I endured the last eight years—honestly. Anyway, you're right, I'm on the run."

"He's abusive?"

"He can be. But it's not exactly him I'm hiding from."

"Then what?"

"I think he paid someone to try to kill me."

Chapter 3

Okay, Hank thought, this was like a movie. Only the woman sitting in front of him, much as she might look like a movie star, wasn't sitting on a set reciting lines. She could be crazy, of course—always a possibility. But something about the way her eyes tightened as she spoke the words made him quite sure she believed what she was saying.

And there was no way on earth he could just walk away from that.

"What happened?" he asked her, knowing he was about to get involved one way or the other. He'd never been one to stand back if someone needed help. Unfortunately.

She shrugged. "It's an old story. Dean mistreated me so I left. I got a lawyer. The lawyer figured I should get a lot of money and went hunting for all of Dean's assets, at least the ones he hadn't already sheltered. Then he notified Dean's lawyer of the amount we were asking for as a settlement."

She drew a long breath. "It was a lot of money. At least I

thought it was. Apparently, Dean did, too, because one night he called me and told me I wouldn't live to collect it."

"You believed him."

She shook her head. "No, honestly, I didn't. I mean, that seemed extreme under any circumstances, even though he'd banged me around a bit. I didn't figure him for a killer." Her blue eyes lifted to his, looking so very sad. "It seems like a huge step from hitting someone when you get mad to actually killing her."

"For most people it would be."

She nodded. "So I didn't even mention it to my lawyer. All I did was tell him I didn't want so much money. But then Dean did this really odd thing."

"What was that?"

"He agreed to the settlement. Without a fight."

"Why do you think that's odd?"

"You'd have to know Dean. He was all about money. But even my lawyer didn't think it was odd. He said Dean had a lot to lose by the publicity from a messy divorce, and probably just wanted it over with."

"That would have been my guess."

Kelly nodded again. "Yeah. That's how it seems. Except I kept remembering him saying I wouldn't live long enough to collect it. But I couldn't put the pieces together. Or maybe I didn't want to put them together."

She stood up suddenly and started pacing the kitchen, rubbing her arms as if she were cold. "I couldn't believe he'd really hurt me, more than hitting and screaming as he'd done before, and while I couldn't believe he'd part with all that money so easily, finally it seemed like my lawyer had to be right. Dean had more to lose by fighting, because it would come out that he'd hit me. And…I'd lived with the man for eight years. As hard as it was to believe he'd accept the settlement, it was harder to believe he would do anything that extreme. In all those years, he only gave me some bruises. That's wrong, but it's not murderous."

She pressed her lips together and closed her eyes. "Regardless…I guess part of me still wanted to believe he was the man I'd fallen in love with. That, after all those years, I really knew him, even his faults, and he couldn't possibly be capable of murder. I believed that right up to the moment some guy grabbed me in the parking garage, stuffed me in his trunk and then tried to drown me."

Hank swore. The kitchen was darkening at last, and now it felt darker with something more than the night. "How'd you get away? Did the cops get him?"

"I'm in good shape and I know some self-defense. I fought hard, and we splashed so much in the water I think he finally got afraid somebody would come. Or maybe that we'd attract an alligator. He gave up and ran."

"My God." He could too easily imagine her terror and desperation. Assuming it was true, of course. "And the police?"

"The cops decided it was a random crime. They didn't think Dean had anything to do with it. Guys who are mad say things like that all the time, they said, especially ones who are being divorced. And I didn't have any proof that Dean was behind it. Maybe he wasn't. My lawyer didn't even think so."

"But you were scared enough to run."

"Yes." She looked at him from haunted eyes. "What kind of lunatic grabs a woman, drives her somewhere and tries to drown her? Without doing anything else? He didn't even empty my wallet. I suppose people like that exist out there, but it just didn't make sense to me. I couldn't risk the possibility Dean had put the guy up to it."

He rubbed his chin, then said gently, "Have you considered that, by running, you might have made it easier for your ex?"

"What do you mean?"

"You already reported to the cops that you thought he was behind the attack. If someone tried to get you again, he'd be the first person they'd look at...unless you were halfway across the country."

"Maybe, but they'd have to prove it. And it won't matter to me if I'm dead, will it?"

He couldn't argue that point.

She came back to the table and sat again. "I could be wrong. I know I could be. But the risk is too great. So I left town with the cash I inherited from my mother and I've been moving ever since. I don't even know if I'll go back for the hearing."

"Do you have to?"

"One of us has to show up. My lawyer thinks Dean won't. So if I don't show up, everything is left hanging out there unfinished. The whole divorce action might even be dismissed, and right now I don't think that's so bad."

"You want to go back to him?" The idea shocked Hank, just from what little she had said.

"No. Never." She sighed again and hugged herself. "I hate even thinking about this. I guess I've been doing it for too long, arguing with myself. The thing is, I already owe my lawyer a ton of money. If I don't get at least part of that settlement, I'm going to spend years trying to pay him off. On the other hand, right now my lawyer isn't willing to lower our settlement demand when Dean has already agreed to it. Apparently, that leaves it all but decided. Nothing left but to make an appearance in court and get the official seal. So I can see his point."

"I can see that, too."

"But if neither of us shows up for the court date, the case will probably be dismissed and we have to start over, and maybe I can persuade my lawyer to basically just bill me for his expenses."

"I see." He did indeed. "Do you feel you're not entitled to some kind of settlement?"

She looked down. "I was mad enough when I left him to want to ruin him. Now I'm just scared. I just want to be free of him and not have to be frightened all the time."

There was nothing Hank could say to that. But he was deeply disturbed by her story. The idea of a man hiring a killer to rid himself of a wife over money wasn't unheard of, but it didn't fit anywhere in the world he lived in. Those were stories you heard, and only rarely, on the news. Hell, as far as he knew, it wasn't even as common as serial killers, although money was surely one of the leading motives for crime.

But what did he know? And her description of what had happened to her did seem strange enough. To kidnap a woman to drown her? Didn't there have to be *some* kind of motive— even a sick one? Although maybe drowning people would be motive enough for one or two freaks out there.

If he was sure of anything, it was that her story was so squirrely he could understand why the cops hadn't believed her.

She could be lying, she could be deluded or she could be right. All three meant he needed to keep an eye on her. And tomorrow he was going to give Ben what-for. Like he needed this?

But then he looked at the woman who sat hunched in the chair across from him and he realized that she *needed* help. Whatever was going on, she needed someone in her life right now. Someone to keep an eye on her.

He doubted he'd ever seen anyone quite as alone as she was. Coming to a strange town where she knew no one because she needed to hide from something real or imagined. That was pretty bad.

He had to find some way to come at this, a way that would reassure her and give him more information about what he needed to do, even if it was just keep an eye on her from a distance.

But how could he do that?

"Anyway," she said finally, giving herself a visible shake, "I should be safe here while I decide if I'm even going back to Miami for the court date. This is the first time I've slowed down in weeks. I've been paying my way with cash. He shouldn't be able to find me."

If someone wanted to kill her, Hank thought, he wouldn't be all that sure she'd covered her tracks well enough. There were a million things a person could do to leave a trail. It all depended on how determined someone was to find her. And he doubted she was very experienced in the kind of thing she'd been trying to do.

He reached for his coffee mug, trying to sort out his thoughts about the best way to handle this. It was possible someone had tried to kill her, strange as it seemed, given the details. He could find out if that was true just by talking to some friends in the Denver Police Department, an inquiry that wouldn't draw any attention here to Conard County.

Looking at the way she was hunched, he felt pretty certain, deep inside, that she had been mugged. Regardless of whether she was correct about why it had happened, he found he *did* believe she'd been attacked. The cops might be right that it had nothing to do with her husband, but that was the question, wasn't it?

Even she didn't seem one hundred percent certain, but he could understand her unwillingness to take any risks: A threat had been made, and then someone had tried to kill her.

He'd heard lots of such threats in his life, often made in moments of anger or stress, that were meaningless. It was usually just a strong expression on the part of people who said it.

On the other hand, if the man—Dean, it was—had felt strongly enough about it to call her and tell her that... Maybe it would be a mistake to dismiss it. Most people said things like that in a moment of passion, not in calmer moments. Not by making a phone call.

He frowned, looking down at his mug because it was easier than looking at her. Looking at her, much as she wasn't his type, reminded him that he was a man with a man's needs, something he had been trying not to think about for a while now.

But looking at the mug didn't help a whole lot, either. It wasn't as if it held any answers.

"What are you thinking?" she asked finally.

"I'm thinking that I'm not quite as prepared to dismiss what you're saying as the police were."

He saw her lift her head, and a flicker of hope appeared on her face before it disappeared.

"That's nice of you," she said finally. "I've been feeling kind of... Well, it's hard to explain. When nobody believes you, you start to wonder if you're losing your mind. It's a very lonely feeling."

He could well imagine it would be. God knew he'd had plenty of reason to second-guess some of his own decisions, and his own interpretations of things.

He still planned to check on whether her mugging story was true, but if it was, he couldn't afford to dismiss the rest. Not when she was living right next door to him.

Not when she apparently didn't have anyone else.

He could almost hear Fran laughing, as once she would have laughed, *Count on you, Hank, to be the one to get the kitten down from the tree.*

"Crap," he said.

"Crap?" Kelly asked.

"Crap," he repeated. Then he regretted it, because she began to shrink in on herself again. "Look, relax. I was just remembering my…a friend. She used to tease me about my inclination to get involved in things, so if you think I'm getting more involved than you want, just tell me to get lost."

"I don't want to do that," she said swiftly. "But you don't have to get involved. Really. I just told you my story. There's no reason for you to give it another thought."

Yeah, there was. Because it might be true. All of it. And that was worth a million reasons right there.

"What were you remembering?" she asked when he said nothing.

Ah, hell. "At the fire department we used to joke about rescuing cats. We did it sometimes—we weren't heartless. But the joke was that you never saw the skeleton of a cat in a tree. Somehow they'd find their ways down, even if we never came to help. Fran, my friend, used to say that I'd always be the first one up into the tree."

"Is that how you see me?"

He saw a spark of anger in her gaze, which was an improvement over her haunted look. "No, actually I don't. It was a comment about me, not you. Not at all about you."

A couple of seconds ticked by, then she relaxed. "Well, it doesn't have to concern you at all. I just told you what happened and why I'm here. I don't need a keeper. Or a rescuer."

"I don't remember saying that you did. You seem to have done all right so far."

At that she seemed to shrink again, and all of a sudden he felt frustrated. "What now?" he asked. "What the hell did I say this time?"

She winced a bit, shaking her head. "It's not you. I just got sick of hearing how I'd done all right for myself by marrying Dean."

"Oh." Kind of an echo. He could understand that. Still, it seemed to him that he and this lady weren't going to get along very well. She seemed to be a walking land mine. Understandable, but not something he especially wanted to deal with. No, he could just keep a general eye out and keep his distance as much as possible. Other than some essential stuff he needed to do around here, there was no need for them to hang out together or anything.

She seemed to have grown fascinated by her coffee mug, both hands wrapped tightly around it as she stared into it. He felt again that sizzle of surprise and attraction he'd felt when first he'd laid eyes on her.

It wasn't just that she was too damn pretty. He ordinarily was drawn to brunettes with warm dark eyes, yet here he was staring at a pale blonde with blue eyes. And yes, she looked like she'd stepped out of Central Casting, or whatever they called it. But there was something else about her, something very *real* and not plastic at all.

It called to him, to his feelings as a man. Kind of like a chest-beating response, he thought wryly. Well, he was long past those days, thanks to becoming pretty well crippled.

Leaning forward, he lifted his cup to sip coffee, trying to find a way to wrap up this conversation that wouldn't leave her feeling abandoned once again. Because whether she was right or not about what had happened, she'd been abandoned by the cops and even by her lawyer. All she had left was herself.

And now him. He sighed, sipped and rose. "Cold," he said by way of explanation. He went to the sink, ignoring the glassy splinters of pain in his hips, dumped the coffee and poured a fresh cup. Then he returned to the table, trying to feel his way.

"I'm sorry," she said suddenly as he sat again. "I didn't mean to cause you so much trouble."

He felt startled. "Trouble? What trouble?"

She hesitated. "Well, renting this place. You obviously weren't ready for a tenant. Now on my account you're rushing things. I've made work for you. And then I went and dragged you in with my story. I could just be crazy. Maybe I should move on."

"I was going to do the work anyway. Speeding it up a bit is no problem. As for you moving on…well, I don't have anything to say about that, but I doubt Ben's going to part with his fee, which is the first month's rent."

"Oh no!" She clapped a hand to her cheek.

"Oh no? That's standard."

"No, no. It's just that I can't believe he rented this place to me knowing I'd only be here a couple of months when he was going to get the first month's rent."

"I can." Hank laughed, relaxing again. Her consternation struck him as cute. "It's okay, really. I just got all worked up about safety issues, but you're a grown-up. You can avoid the stuff I was worried about. And things like the stove can be fixed quickly. Nothing's changed, except the order in which I was going to do repairs."

"Are you sure?"

"Absolutely." He waved at the floors. "I was going to get to these next, but since you're here, I'll just rearrange my schedule. No big deal. First the stove, then the electrician."

"Why were you going to do the floors first?"

"Because they annoy the hell out of me." He was still smiling. And because they sometimes tripped him, when his leg was acting up and he didn't lift his foot high enough. But he didn't want to bring his disability up. Bad enough living with it, without having buckets of sympathy ladled his way.

"Well, can I help with them? I need something to do

besides sit around all day worrying about what might never happen."

And that, he thought, was a healthy attitude. He felt his last reservations about her start slipping away. "Sure. I'd like that. Help is always welcome."

From the way she beamed, he realized how much she wanted to feel useful again.

But even as he watched her, he saw her smile start to slip, and a look of horror began to replace it.

"Kelly? Kelly, what's wrong?"

"I just realized something. I can't believe I was too stupid to think of it before."

"What's that?"

"The place where the guy tried to drown me? It was in one of the canals around Miami."

"So the gators would get you?"

"Maybe." But then she shook her head. "No, it just suddenly struck me it was a canal where I went jogging a lot of mornings. Not too far from Dean's house."

He wasn't sure where she was leading. "That would seem stupid. It could link it to Dean."

She shook her head. "Don't you see? He would have made it look like I might have fallen while I was out running. And there are gators in those canals. Lots of them. Bull sharks, too, in some places. There wouldn't be much evidence for long. But the important thing is, how likely is it that someone who didn't know me would know where I liked to jog?"

She had him there. Hard. All of a sudden, no matter how wacky it might have sounded at first, he believed her husband wanted her dead.

"Okay," he said quietly, feeling his jaw tighten. "I'm buying it. All of it."

She lifted her gaze, questioning without words.

"I wasn't sure at first. It seems so far-fetched that the guy would want to kill you. I mean, I know it happens, but it doesn't happen that often, does it?"

"I don't know."

"Me, either. But to me it seems a helluva lot more likely that you were mugged by some stranger, odd as it seems, than that he'd carry you out some place just to drown you. But if he took you to a canal where you liked to jog…"

"He could just have been watching me," she said tautly.

"Sure. Then why not go for you while you were out for a run? Why stalk you to your parking garage, then take you back there to kill you? Did he try to rape you or anything?"

She shook her head. "He just hit me over the head."

"And you said he didn't rob you, either. That fits with trying to make it look like an accident."

Much to his dismay, he watched one lone tear roll down her cheek.

"Why are you crying?" he asked. "Isn't this what you already thought was going on?"

She drew a shaky breath. "I guess," she said sadly, "that some part of me wanted to believe I was wrong. Somewhere deep inside, I wanted to believe I was wrong about Dean. I wanted to believe I was making a mountain out of a molehill. I wanted to believe it was just random. Dammit, Hank, I didn't want to believe, *really* believe, that the man I married is capable of murder."

"You believed it enough to run."

"And I spent the last six weeks telling myself I was crazy, even though I kept running."

"And now you don't feel crazy anymore."

She shook her head. "Not now."

"The canal changed your mind?"

"Yes, it did. Because Dean knew I ran out there all the time. Everyone knew it. And when they got around to finding whatever pieces of me were left after the gators or sharks were done, it would have been a sad, sad accident. Except that someone tried to drown me in that canal."

"The police should have listened to that part." He felt his ire stirring.

"How could they when I didn't tell them? I was half-hysterical over being attacked, I was accusing Dean, they were telling me it was just random... God, I can't believe I didn't put it together before!"

He could. He knew what shock and denial could do to a mind. He'd experienced enough of his own. Impulsively, he reached out and took her hand, giving it a quick squeeze before he let go.

Of all the damn times to be inappropriately aware of the satin of a woman's skin, this was it. He shoved the awareness down into a pit for later consideration. There were more important issues to deal with.

"You didn't want to believe it any more than the cops and your lawyer did," he said after a moment. "That's normal enough. I doubt I'd have felt any differently."

"No." She shivered and rubbed her arms again. The night was cooling down, but not that much. At least not for him, but he didn't come from Miami. "Jeez, now I *do* feel crazy. I went on the run because it occurred to me that Dean had paid someone to kill me, but I didn't think of the one thing that proved it until just now? I need a shrink."

"No," he said firmly, "you're normal. I don't think the normal human mind is designed to readily accept the idea that someone wants to kill us. Certainly not someone we think we know and used to love."

"Maybe. Maybe." But she sounded awfully doubtful.

"Anyway," he said bracingly, "you're safe here. That's what matters."

"Yes. It is." Several minutes ticked by then she managed

a wan smile. "That was the whole point in coming here. But now I've got a lot of other stuff to think about."

"Such as?"

"Such as why I've been such an idiot, believing and not believing, and running if I didn't fully believe it, and…"

"Whoa," he said gently, smiling for her. "Don't start beating yourself up. The mind works in its own ways, and sometimes we don't realize things until we're ready for them."

She seemed willing to accept that. When he went home a half hour later, the conversation had even turned back to the home repair project she wanted to involve herself in.

She seemed happier. And he was determined to find out what the hell had happened in Miami.

Thank God for friends in the police department.

Because, if he emerged from his own denial to look at this clearly, it seemed entirely possible that if a man with money really wanted to find her, there was little to stop him.

He needed details. Every one he could get. Only then could he figure out what he could do, what he might need to do.

He headed straight for his computer to send an email.

Chapter 4

The next few days passed swiftly for Kelly. She seemed to have put Dean and his machinations out of her mind, at least for now, because she was busy, truly busy, for the first time since she'd gone on the run.

It helped to give Hank a hand with the stove, to hover around while the electrician solved what turned out to be relatively minor problems.

Repairing the termite damage in the basement was messier and much more time-consuming, but she enjoyed the hands-on work of helping to jack up joists and reinforce the damaged ones. She especially enjoyed using the hammer to pound nails.

At one point her enjoyment must have become evident because Hank laughed.

"What's so funny?"

"You look like you're hammering Dean's head."

At once she blushed. "I wouldn't do that. But it's nice to work out some anger."

"Especially harmlessly. Hammer away, lady. Need more nails?"

She laughed and took a few more nails from him, tucking them into the already-heavy pockets of the canvas work apron he'd given her.

"This feels so good," she admitted when they decided to break for lunch.

"What does?"

"Doing something again. Accomplishing something. Spending all my time riding buses and hiding in motel rooms…well, that's just not me. I like to be busy."

"So do I, which is why I took on this house. I grew up next door, and the people who owned it were like grandparents to me. When I came back for their funerals, it just killed me to see how the place was falling apart. And then I moved back and I figured it would be a great way to keep myself busy between stints on the range."

"There's plenty to do here," she agreed.

He locked up the house behind them, and she walked next door with him. Already she'd gotten used to the fact that he insisted on making her lunch if she was going to help him with the repairs.

She liked it. There was an easiness in Hank's manner that appealed to her even more than his rugged good looks. He might limp, he might look as if pain never left him, but he was still easy to be with, as if he was comfortable with who he was. Which was more than she could say.

Oh, don't go there again, she told herself. But her thoughts refused to listen to reason. Somehow, sitting across a table from Hank while they ate tuna sandwiches, having spent the morning working with him, made him feel like an intimate. Closer than her girlfriends during the years of her marriage.

She had the worst urge to tell him about all the nagging self-doubts and criticisms she kept leveling at herself, even though she knew she was probably being too harsh.

But considering the mess her life had turned into, being harsh with herself didn't seem all that extreme.

"I was an idiot," she announced.

"What makes you say that?" His gray eyes were steady, not quite smiling, as he looked at her over his sandwich.

"Oh, I've had a lot of time to think about the last eight years. I made a lot of mistakes."

"Mistakes," he said, "are only bad if we don't learn from them."

"Right. I tell myself that all the time. I've got a lot to learn from."

"We all do."

It wasn't a question, and she appreciated that. Since the first night, he'd been awfully careful about not questioning her about anything that wasn't immediately in front of them. Maybe he was respecting her privacy, or maybe he didn't want to know. Either way, she liked that he didn't push her to places she didn't want to go.

But now she felt like talking a bit. It had been a long time since she had felt she could confide in anyone. And Hank seemed safe, both from his manner and the fact that she wouldn't be here long.

"You know," she remarked, "it's sad, but I didn't even feel like I could trust my girlfriends with the things I was dealing with and trying to sort out."

"Then they couldn't have been good friends."

"I guess not." She put her sandwich down. "Or maybe sometimes it's just easier to talk to a stranger."

He lifted a brow, but didn't say anything, merely taking another bite of his sandwich. She liked the way weather and sun had created fine little creases around his eyes, the way his face was sun-browned right up to the line where his hat often sat.

She looked at his hands. They were big and work-roughened, unlike the last hands that had touched her. She wondered what it would feel like to have those hands on her skin, rather than Dean's soft ones.

"Dean was vain about his hands," she said suddenly.

Hank glanced down at his. "Uh… Sorry, I'm not."

"No need to be sorry. I was just noticing that your hands look like they do hard work. Dean protected his hands in every way possible. I suppose that was because he was a surgeon. They were his instruments, in a way. I just accepted it, although I have to admit I found it odd the first time I saw him lather them with moisturizer and wear gloves to bed."

Hank's eyes widened a shade, and something like a stifled laugh escaped him. "Really?"

"Really." She half smiled. "I mean, I suppose it was necessary. He had to touch his patients, and most of them were wealthy women who wanted to look a lot younger. He couldn't be scratching them with dry skin and calluses. And surgical soaps, as he often complained, were hard on the skin. Dried it out."

Hank nodded. "Okay, I can see why he'd take care of his hands."

"Me, too. But every week he had a manicure, too. He was the first man I ever knew who did that."

"I guess a lot of men do that. Not that I know any, but I've heard of it."

"Sure. There are probably lots of fields where taking good care of your hands makes a good impression."

"You're making me want to hide mine."

She laughed and shook her head. "No, no! Don't. I like your hands. I just noticed the contrast, that's all. But I've been thinking about Dean a lot, obviously, and about how it all

happened and the things I should have noticed and didn't…"
She trailed off, feeling the darkness edge in again. She didn't
want it, didn't want to let it take hold. She was safe now. At
least for now.

"Hindsight is 20/20 and all that," Hank remarked. "I
sometimes think the worst curse of being human is that
we actually remember things, especially the things we did
wrong."

She saw his face tighten a shade, then relax as if he'd
pushed something away. More than ever she wondered if he
had a story, too. But she didn't know how to ask.

"So, Dean's care of his hands didn't put you off?" he asked.
"Do you think it should have?"

"No. Just one of those odd things that pops into your head
sometimes. I was so naive."

"Really?"

"Yeah, really. I went to work in Dean's office right after I
finished my associate's degree in medical billing. He hired
me on the spot."

Something in Hank's gaze seemed to indicate that he
understood why, and she flushed again. "I know. It was my
looks. They were so important to him."

"How so?"

"Oh, he was forever on me to look my best. No slouching
around in old sweats or jeans. Nope. From the minute I got
out of the shower in the morning, I had to be perfectly made
up and perfectly dressed."

He cocked a brow. "I don't see any makeup on you now,
and you look fine to me. Better than fine actually."

"Thanks." She felt her cheeks heat again. Darn, when was
the last time she had blushed so often? "But it's superficial. I
learned that a long time ago."

"How so?"

"I won the lottery when it comes to looks. I know that. But

my mom always taught me that looks fade. It's what's on the inside that lasts."

"Your mom was right."

Kelly nodded. "Of course she was. We seem to be using a lot of platitudes."

"They seem to fit."

She gave another little laugh. "Yeah."

"They're probably platitudes because they're true. Trite is usually true, too. At least that's how it seems to me. So back to Dean and your looks."

"Well, I feel stupid now that I didn't understand why he was so interested in me from the moment I started working for him. I mean, lots of his patients are beautiful women so it never seemed to me that he would notice my looks."

"Maybe it takes some of the shine off when you know you created that beauty."

Kelly gasped, astonished by the thought, and then burst into a gale of laughter. "You might be right," she managed breathlessly through the laughs. "You might be right."

"Of course I'm right," he said, spreading his arms as if to invite approval. "So you were beautiful, young and naive, and ever so much better to squire around on his arm than someone older whose surgical details he knew so intimately. I mean, imagine looking at a woman and remembering every detail of her face-lift."

Kelly clapped a hand to her mouth. "Oh my... Oh!" The image was at once horrifying and terribly funny.

"Frankenstein's bride," Hank said, shrugging. "That's how it would strike me, anyway."

"I never thought of that!" She dabbed at the corners of her eyes, wiping at the tears of laughter. "You're great, Hank. I swear that thought never crossed my mind."

He smiled crookedly. "It was the first one that occurred to me. So okay, you were what, twenty?"

She nodded.

"And you were fresh meat. No surgical memories attached, and you had the kind of beauty that would make other men drool."

Her laughter faded. "I know. It took me a while to realize why he was interested. It was just so flattered that he paid special attention to me, and even more flattered when he asked me out. I fell hook, line and sinker."

"I imagine it would be easy to do."

"That bothers me—that I was so easy. That I fell for it. I guess I was just blinded. I couldn't imagine any reason for him to notice me other than that he really liked me. His office was full of beautiful women. What I didn't realize was what a trophy I'd be."

"How old is he?"

"That's the thing," she said. "Too old. That should have been another tip-off. What could a twenty-year-old girl have to say or do that would interest a man who was nearly fifty? Other than sex, I mean. I should have guessed."

"I guess you weren't used to swimming with barracudas."

Startled, she started to smile again. "No, I guess I wasn't. I expected people to be honest. It took a few years of living with him to realize that most people *aren't* honest. At least not in those circles. They're all about appearances. And for a while, I'm sorry to say, so was I."

"We tend to adopt the values of the people around us."

"I was raised with better values," she protested. "Much better values. So I look back and think what an idiot I was. Blinded by flattery, and money, and moving in circles that I thought only movie stars moved in."

"Try the youth excuse."

"It's not sitting very well just now."

He shook his head and reached for his sandwich, taking

another bite. "You wouldn't be the first person who'd trusted the wrong people, and got her head turned for a while. I take it the honeymoon didn't last long?"

"It did for a while. A few years, actually. At first I didn't realize how controlling he was because everything was so new to me. I just did what I was told. But eventually it began to get to me. I couldn't even decide what to wear without his approval. And after a few years I began to get my own sense of what I could do and what I shouldn't do in those circles. I began to realize that I was capable of choosing my own outfit for a party or whatever."

"And that's when the trouble began."

She nodded, compressing her lips. "It all seems so clear now. I just wonder how I could have been blind to it for so long."

"Apparently, despite his best efforts, he didn't turn you into a windup doll."

"No." She sighed and shook her head. "Not quite." Looking down she realized that she had hardly touched her sandwich, and that her stomach was rumbling. She was being rude not to eat the meal he'd provided, and she would get awfully hungry as they worked that afternoon if she ate nothing.

She picked it up and forced herself to take a bite, even though it now tasted almost like sawdust. "I think," she said when she swallowed, "I've just told you more about the last eight years than I've told anyone else."

"It's hard to talk to people who keep telling you how lucky you are."

She looked at him. "Where did you get that from?"

"From something you said your first night here. Something about how you did all right for yourself."

"Oh, that. Yeah, I heard a lot of that."

"That makes it kind of hard to complain."

"It does." And somehow she sensed that he knew that

intimately. But she was afraid to say anything, to ask anything. These moments were precious for her because she'd finally been able to talk to someone besides herself, and she didn't want to shatter the moments of intimacy by barging into things he'd prefer to have left alone.

But the man was a mystery. That much was becoming clear to her.

Then another thought occurred to her. "I probably should apologize for dumping all that on you." And she should probably be embarrassed for exposing herself so much to a stranger. What was it about him that made her run on about things she'd kept securely locked inside her own head?

It's not as if he was a therapist or anything.

"I don't mind listening," he said as he finished his sandwich. "I was just sitting here thinking how easy it is for us to make the kind of mistakes you're talking about. I've made my own share. The thing is, you shouldn't beat yourself up for what you can look back and see now. You sure didn't see it back then."

"No, I didn't. But I keep thinking I should have."

He smiled slightly, but it crinkled the corners of his eyes. "Tell me what little girl didn't grow up hoping Prince Charming would find her at the ball."

His words struck her, making her catch her breath. "You think that's what it was?"

"I think that story is probably at the back of every girl's mind—consciously or not. And it's understandable. Maybe Prince Charming won't be rich, maybe he won't ride a white horse or whatever, but I'm sure most little girls think their prince is going to come. So there you were, the handsome, wealthy doctor showered you with attention. No reason to think it was about your beauty, because, as you said, he was surrounded by beautiful women. Why would you stick out for him? Because you were young? Partly. Because you weren't his work product? I'm sure. Then there's this whole power thing a guy feels with a much younger beauty on his arm. But you were just twenty and your dreams seemed to be coming true. Why would you be looking under rocks for his midlife crisis?"

"Wow." She breathed the word. Then she felt a huge rush of warmth toward him. "Thanks, Hank. You're a nice guy. A really nice guy."

"Why? Because I can see that a young, naive girl was hornswoggled by an older, much more experienced man with a bunch of personal issues? The thing to keep reminding yourself, Kelly, is why you married him. Was it for love, or was it for his money?"

"I loved him," she said. "I really thought I loved him. At the time I'd have married him if he hadn't had a dime."

"Then I guess you don't have one damn thing to apologize for." He paused. "Didn't he have you sign a prenup?"

"Prenuptial agreement? No, he never even suggested it."

His face darkened. "Then it's entirely possible he never intended to let you leave that marriage. At least not alive."

Sometimes a thought just wouldn't leave you alone. And from the instant that Hank had mentioned a prenuptial agreement—so common these days—and learned that Dean had never suggested it, his mind went to places so dark he was surprised they even existed inside him.

Given her description of Dean's controlling behavior, the lack of a prenup stood out like a flashing warning sign on a lonely road. The man was old enough, and controlling enough, that he wouldn't have overlooked such a thing unless he was sure Kelly would never be able to take him to the cleaners in court. Because Hank found it hard to believe that Dean had been anywhere near as in love as Kelly had been. She was right: Other than sex, why would a twenty-year-old appeal to a man of his age, experience and stature?

He had wanted a trophy wife, and he hadn't felt any need to protect himself financially from divorce, alimony or settlements. That either meant he felt he'd sheltered enough of his assets, or it meant he'd been sure he could get rid of her if she became a problem.

Given what Kelly had said, it appeared Dean had been sure he could get rid of her.

He hobbled into his tiny den and sat at his computer to check his email. At last there was a response from his friend in the Denver PD. Yup, there'd been a report filed about a mugging involving Kelly Scanlon Devereaux—so she hadn't given him her married name, only her maiden name. Smart. Maybe. Or maybe not.

The report listed it as a kidnapping and mugging at canalside, detailing streets and intersections that meant nothing to Hank, and physical injuries: mild concussion from a blow to the head and some bruising. He skipped the photos taken of Kelly and tried to glean more information.

The description of the mugger was vague. The cops accurately reported that he'd snatched her from her parking garage, and that she'd claimed that her husband might have tried to have her killed.

Just the cold, hard facts. There'd been a bulletin put out to look for a man who met Kelly's description, but no one had yet been found. Kelly would probably be astonished to know that the cops had even interviewed Dean, who apparently had expressed the proper amount of horror because it was noted that the investigating officers had no reason to suspect him. Basically, nothing Kelly hadn't already told him.

His friend in Denver had appended his own thoughts. "Just so you know, accusations like this aren't rare, but they almost never pan out. Most likely the cops told Devereaux that he'd better hope nothing happened to his wife because he'd be at the top of their suspect list. I've said that a few times myself. Just to be safe."

Just as he would have expected. Devereaux had been warned that they were looking at him. Unfortunately, that might be a bad thing, depending on the kind of man Dean was. Most folks who intended no harm would stay miles away from the victim after a warning like that. Other people, however, might just want to get even and finish it. And Kelly's going on the run would make it even easier, because who would put it together if she were now to die in an out-of-the-way town in Wyoming?

Nobody, that's who. Nobody at all.

And now it might even be easier, because while it would have to look like an accident in Miami, here in Conard City it wouldn't have to.

He leaned back in his chair, ignoring the grinding-glass sensation in his hip, and turned it all around in his mind. The blackness that filled him was not unlike the blackness that had filled him when he'd finally awakened after his last fire and learned what had happened.

Or maybe in some way it was even worse this time, because this time he had advance warning.

Tomorrow, he promised himself, he was going to find out just how many breadcrumbs Kelly might have left behind her. Because he was sure she had left some.

And then, dammit, he was going to hunt down Ben and find out what the hell he'd been doing renting the house in that condition.

But even as he sat there, Hank knew. Her beauty. Her aura of vulnerability. It would take a far better man than Ben to say no to that blond, blue-eyed beauty.

He cussed quietly, and closed his eyes, trying to tamp down

the response his body insisted on giving him every time he thought of Kelly or glanced at her.

He'd probably go to sleep tonight and dream of her. Sexual dreams. Because he wanted her—no two ways about it. Straight, simple, basic. Lust.

She deserved better than that.

But he was going to dream about her anyway, because his body was making demands and sending powerful signals to his brain.

He guessed that meant in some way he was no better than Dean Devereaux. No better at all.

Disgusted, he poured himself a shot of bourbon and tried to think of something else. Anything else.

Because he already despised himself enough.

Chapter 5

Kelly felt sick to her stomach. Thinking over her conversation with Hank had only made her more frightened. That thing he'd said about the prenup—he was right. She knew how attached Dean was to money and all the power and prestige it gave him.

So that lack of a prenup probably meant exactly what Hank had said—that Dean had been sure he would never face her in divorce court.

She might not have a medical background, but after eight years of working in a medical practice, she had some idea of how easily a doctor could arrange for something to go wrong.

But, of course, Dean wouldn't do it himself. She was young and healthy, not a patient on his table. But she wouldn't doubt that somewhere in the back of his mind was the knowledge of how easy it would have been to remove her later in life, whether because he wanted a younger trophy wife or she just became a problem.

For a long time she hadn't been a problem, and that sickened her, too. Stars in her eyes, her mother would have said. Her mother would have been right. She'd been so overwhelmed, so awed, so in love, so dazzled…she'd been as compliant as a doll. All she wanted to do was please Dean. Keep him happy, make him proud of his wife.

Perfectly natural. And the women around her, all in similar boats, had pretty much reinforced that attitude.

At some point, though, she had begun to feel that she was trading too much to keep Dean happy. Why should it matter whether she wore the red dress or the blue one? Why should it matter if she went a half hour at breakfast without makeup if no one else was going to see her?

First had come the yelling. He said things that wounded her so badly she hadn't dared fight back. Things that made her afraid to risk riling him again. Things that cut away at her self-confidence. Things that had made her meek and eager to please him, rather than face his wrath.

Her friends were more cynical about their relationships with their wealthy husbands. They knew they were making a trade-off: security in exchange for being beautiful and compliant. Many of them had even become Dean's patients at a rather young age, worrying about every little line or slight sag in their bodies.

But Kelly hadn't gotten cynical. At first she just told herself that Dean worked hard, that he was a gifted artist in the medical profession. Naturally, he was a bit temperamental— many surgeons were—and what did it cost her, after all, to do everything the way he wanted?

But finally, over the last two years, when he'd gone past yelling at her to hitting her, some spark had awakened in her. Some realization that the man didn't love her. That to him she was an object—no better than a dog. Maybe not even as important. Dean, she finally realized, didn't care one whit about what Kelly might want or need. She was just another possession.

Unlike her friends, she didn't think it was enough to attend swank parties, eat at the best restaurants, play golf and tennis in her free time. Maybe because she had never stopped working in Dean's office.

In retrospect, it seemed odd that he hadn't turned her into a housewife, but maybe he liked being sure he could control her every minute of the day. Or maybe her presence at the office protected him from embarrassing moments with some of his patients. God knew, she'd seen enough of them look at him with hunger once he'd transformed them into the beauties they wanted to be.

She'd never wondered about it. It just was. Dean coddled the women who came to him, made them feel as if each of them was his most important patient while he charged them through the nose and their wealthy husbands paid for it.

So, of course, they mistook his bedside manner for something more. One thing she knew for sure about him—he never got mixed up with patients. His staff maybe, but never his patients.

Finally, during those last few months, around the third time he hit her, she had started taking a course in self-defense. And she didn't tell him about it. All she knew was that she was determined to get to the point where if he ever hit her again she could protect herself.

But it hadn't gotten to that point. The last time he hit her, something in her snapped. As soon as he'd gone out for his golf game in the morning, she had packed a few things and left.

Enough.

And now this. Now she was truly frightened. Oh, she tried to tell herself that she'd run long enough and far enough that he could never find her, but some part of her couldn't be sure.

Some part of her no longer felt safe. Probably the same part of her that no longer fully trusted her own judgment about things.

After all, if she could have been so wrong about Dean, how could she know what else she was wrong about?

No prenup. Those words chilled her. She so feared that Hank was right. Dean, so canny about financial matters, so careful about feathering his nest and increasing his wealth, wouldn't have overlooked something like that.

And if she'd remained compliant, they might well have lived out another thirty years just the same way.

God. She shuddered just thinking about it.

She had been on her way to becoming a Stepford Wife. So close. Closing her eyes, she wondered what it was that had awakened her from the spell.

Because when she looked back, she honestly couldn't understand any of it at all.

Hank had plenty to think about come morning, and it wasn't all about working on the house next door, although he really needed to finish caulking the new windows before it rained.

No, he was thinking about Kelly, as he seemed to be doing entirely too much lately. Now that his male urges had been fully awakened, he found his thoughts too often drifting to her, and his eyes too often drifting over her body.

She had a cute rump as she knelt on the floor working at pulling away old vinyl tiles.

He'd considered just laying fresh vinyl over the old, but when he looked at the torn, ragged and tacked-down stuff, he couldn't bring himself to leave it. Especially since he was sure there was wood under it, although he had no idea what condition it was in.

But this house was old enough that it probably had been built with solid wood floors, unlike newer houses that were built with cheap subflooring meant to be covered by carpet.

What was the worst that could happen, he wondered, as he tugged at the vinyl himself. That refinishing wouldn't salvage it all? That he'd have to replace it with laminate, which people seemed to prefer these days anyway?

Then his gaze drifted back to Kelly. Her arms were bare as she worked and he could see muscles bunching, a sign of a lot of exercise of one kind or another. She took care of herself. Whether she had done it because she wanted to or because her husband had demanded it, he had no idea, but he'd already figured out that she wasn't afraid of hard work, and he liked that.

Along with the way she looked, of course. It was impossible not to see her stretch and reach and crouch and just generally move without thinking about how all that loveliness would feel in his arms, against his body, writhing above him or below him.

He was too young still to be turning into a dirty old man, wasn't he? But of course, these weren't dirty-old-man thoughts. They were the normal thoughts of a fairly healthy male when surrounded by a beautiful woman's presence and scents.

Desperate to get his mind off the fact that there was a bed only a few dozen feet away, he came back to something that concerned him.

"How sure are you that you didn't leave a trail?" he asked.

At that she stopped pulling at the tile. For a couple of seconds she froze, then she turned to face him, sitting on her butt, legs stretched out, her arms propping her from behind. An unfortunate choice of position from his perspective, since it seemed to accentuate her breasts. Full, perfect breasts, from what he could tell, not too big, not to small.

He closed his eyes a moment and silently yelled at himself.

"Truthfully," she said finally, "I'm not sure."

His eyes snapped open. "What do you mean?"

"Exactly that. I'm not sure. I mean, I thought I was being very careful. But these days you can't always get by without showing ID."

Too true, he thought. He knew all the new precautions from Homeland Security. "I know. You practically can't use a public restroom anymore."

At that she smiled faintly, but it didn't quite reach her eyes. "I thought buses would be pretty anonymous, and mostly they were. I paid cash for my tickets, but sometimes they wanted ID anyway. Not every time, just some of the time. Then there were motels. The really, really bad ones just let you sign in, but you'd be surprised how hard they are to find. So sometimes I had to use ID there too."

"Did they write it down?"

"A few times."

"Phone calls?"

"I only made a few, to my lawyer. He should be safe enough."

"He should."

His knees and hips were hurting, so he tried sitting cross-legged. Didn't help much, but little did. "Okay, so you weren't completely off the grid."

"No, but I think, I hope, things were scattered enough that I'd be hard to follow. It wasn't like I was making a beeline in some direction. I just bounced this way and that."

"Smart." But maybe not smart enough. "Where was the last place you showed your ID?"

"To Ben, when I rented this place."

He swore. Shoveling his hand into his breast pocket, he pulled out his cell phone. "Ben, this is Hank Jackson," he said to voice mail. "Get your ass over to my rental house now."

Kelly's eyes had widened. "He wouldn't have done anything with the information, would he? He said it was just for skip-tracing if I didn't pay my rent."

"I don't know. But I'm going to find out anyway." Seeing the fright in her gaze, he tried to be soothing. "There's no reason he should have done anything with the information. I mean, you paid cash, right?"

"Yes, I did. He just made a photocopy of my license and said he wouldn't need it as long as I kept paying rent."

Kelly jumped up from the floor and started pacing. "This is awful, Hank. Maybe I should just get on a bus again."

"The problem," he said tautly, "is one you already pointed out. People keep wanting ID from you. So if someone is looking for you, it all comes down to whether you can stay one jump ahead. And since you've been here for a few days now, you've already lost some of your jump. Assuming Ben did a background check on you. If he didn't show your info to anyone, you're still ahead of the game. Where was the last place you had to use it?"

Her face seemed almost white as she looked at him. "In Laramie."

Too close for comfort. Too damn close. He had a sudden urge to hammer his fist on something, and call himself all kinds of names. First he hadn't believed her. Then he'd checked on her background. Of course, he had thought it would be safe to check through a friend in Denver. After all, Denver was a big place, and far enough away not to pinpoint this town. But Denver and then Laramie could narrow a search quite a bit. Too much maybe.

"You're gonna hate me," he said.

She stopped pacing and looked at him with some amazement. "Why?"

"I emailed a friend on the Denver Police Department to check into your mugging."

She froze, and if anything she grew paler. "Why?" she asked hoarsely.

"Because I wanted to know what they'd done. What had happened."

"Because you didn't trust me."

"I mostly *did* trust you. I just…needed to know."

Her face tightened until she almost looked old. "You didn't believe me." Flat, unemotional. Cold. "Well, of course, why would you? Even I know how crazy it sounds." Now her voice began to rise. "So you let them know I was near here?"

"I didn't let anyone know. I just asked him to check on the mugging. And on what the cops did. And Denver is hours from here. It's not like I went to the local police. I could have done that."

"Yeah. Right." She started to glare, but the glare quickly flashed over to panic. "I've got to get out of here now. Get on a bus and get out of here." She began to look around wildly, like a frightened rabbit. "I can't stay here! How could you do that after what I told you?"

Ignoring the pain, he shoved himself to his feet. "Kelly, listen. I asked my friend to be discreet, and I'm sure he was. There's no reason to think your husband could access a request between police departments for information."

"There's no reason to think a lot of things, like that he would try to have me killed. My God, Hank, I trusted you!"

That cut. That really cut. But what cut most of all was that she was right. Some niggling sense of disbelief had made him check her story out. And because of that there was a possibility, however remote, that he'd led a killer closer.

"Don't you get it, Hank? Dean has money. Lots of money. The kind of money that can buy information. Hell, he probably wouldn't even have to pay for it. He could just call the cops and say he's worried because I disappeared, and then some nice police officer could tell him there'd been an inquiry about me from Denver. Do you honestly think that couldn't happen?"

He clenched his fists, furious at himself. But he was also a little angry with her. "It would have been meaningless if you hadn't given ID in Laramie."

"Are you going to blame me?"

The anger drained from him as if a balloon had been punctured. "No. I'm not blaming you. God knows, I'm not blaming you. I'm blaming myself."

That seemed to draw her up short. Some of the tightness left her face. "No," she said after a moment. "No. There's no point in blaming yourself. I know how crazy it all sounded. There were plenty of times I thought I was crazy myself. But now…now I think I'd better pack."

That ripped at him somehow. Without thinking, he reached out and caught her arm gently. "No," he said.

"No? What if Ben did a background on me? They'll find me. Am I supposed to sit here like a half-dead duck?"

He shook his head. "No, that's not what I mean. What I mean is, here you have someone who'll look out for you. If the guy traces you here, you won't be alone. But what about the next town where they want your ID? And the next? I think I should talk to the sheriff. And then I think you shouldn't be alone again, not until this divorce thing is settled."

He could see the struggle on her face, see the yearning

not to be alone with her fear battling an equal, if not greater, terror of being alone.

"I don't know," she said finally on a breath. "I don't know."

He dared to step closer, still holding her arm gently. "You don't have to face this alone," he said firmly. "I may be just a cowboy, but I can help."

Slowly her blue eyes lifted to his again. "Why do you keep saying you're just a cowboy?"

"Because that's what I am, now, and I'm happy with it."

Then she said something that tore at his heart. "I'd like to be happy with who I am, someday. Right now, that someday looks a long way away."

"It may be closer than you think."

"If I can survive the next couple of months."

He hesitated, then gave up his last shred of resistance. Fran had been right. He always went up into the tree. "I'll help you," he said. "Whatever it takes."

Though he made the promise sincerely, only moments later he mentally kicked himself, wondering if he were a grade-A jackass. Look at him, crippled with pain and unreliable legs. What was he doing holding himself out as a protector?

Maybe setting himself up for another terrible failure, like going into that burning building. Another terrible loss on his conscience.

He almost took the promise back, qualified it, warned her that he wasn't the strongest person to rely on.

But it wasn't in him. The woman needed help, and he didn't see anyone else around to stand in round the clock.

Always the first one up into the tree. His downfall. He just hoped like hell it wouldn't be Kelly's as well.

Kelly was horrified to feel herself crumbling. The kindness of this man, his willingness to take on her problem, his words of concern… God, it had been so long since she felt that anyone at all really cared about her. The caring weakened her, and tears came to her eyes.

The next thing she knew, she was wrapped securely in strong arms, and pressed comfortingly against a hard chest. A hand stroked her hair awkwardly, and a rough voice murmured soothingly.

"Somehow we'll deal with this, Kelly."

We. The world's most beautiful word. It opened up a great gaping wound in her that she hadn't even realized existed until that moment. To have someone actually care.

"You don't have to," she said brokenly, although there was nothing she wanted more in the world than not to be alone. "I can just go back to hiding."

"Shh," he said. "We'll start taking major precautions to protect you. But if you still really want to run, well…I'll go with you."

Astonishment rippled through her. This man, this cowboy, had just offered to uproot himself and go wandering to protect a woman he hardly knew. How many people like that could there possibly be in the world? Surely they were few and far between. She hadn't met anyone before who would make an offer like that.

Inevitably, she thought about what it would be like to go on the run with him. He'd use his own ID, not hers, and she had enough left from her inheritance to pay for both of them so it wouldn't be a financial burden on him.

But then she realized two things. First, it would be unfair to ask that of anyone. And second, she was sick to death of running. That's why she'd rented this ramshackle house in the first place. Yes, she thought she would be safe here, but she'd also been so tired of running. So very tired.

Two more months of buses and hitchhiking and seedy motels? Always looking over her shoulder? She couldn't do that anymore. She just couldn't. It had been awful in every sense of the word. Constantly feeling like a hare just ahead of the hounds, death on her heels somewhere but no idea just where, the filthy motel rooms where she hadn't even wanted to take off her clothes, the Laundromats that slowed down her flight and made her feel exposed, the grabbing of quick food at a lunch counter to eat as she kept on running?

Her stomach tightened into a painful knot at the thought, and then the pain wrapped like a noose around her throat until she could barely breathe. It hit her—all of it—in an instant, and she started to sob, except she couldn't quite get breath around the garrote that seemed to squeeze her throat.

"Breathe," Hank said sharply. He held her a few inches away. "Breathe, Kelly."

Her head seemed to be swimming. She hardly felt the hot tears rolling down her cheeks. He gave her another shake, and it seemed to loosen her throat enough to suck in a huge, painful breath.

"That's better," he said soothingly, and pulled her close again. "I won't let anyone hurt you, okay? Just try to let go of the panic."

She dragged in another breath, and the tightness began to ease. Just a bit. But the tears continued to flow as if they'd been held behind a dam that was now crumbling. She hadn't cried much since she'd left Dean. Not even after the attack. Until this moment she hadn't even realized that she had *wanted* to cry.

"I just thought of something," he said as he patted her shoulder and rubbed her back.

"What?" The word barely squeezed out.

"You gave your ID in Laramie before my friend in Denver requested info from Miami. That should lead this guy in exactly the wrong direction."

"Yeah. If there *is* a guy."

"Stop that. You've been doing the right thing. You can't afford to just assume it was a random mugging. You're right about that. Better safe than sorry, as they say. I'm with you on that. If that means running, just know one thing. I'm not letting you run alone."

Her tears turned to hiccups, the sobs that hadn't been able to escape. "No. I can't ask that of you."

"You didn't ask. I offered."

"Still." She tipped her wet face up and looked at him, thinking that for some inexplicable reason in just a few short days his face had become the most beautiful she'd ever seen. Just looking at him eased some deep pain inside her. "If you think I can be safe here, I'll stay. I can't face it again, Hank. It was awful, just awful."

"I can imagine."

"That's part of the reason I decided to stay here. I couldn't take it anymore. I needed a break."

"Perfectly understandable." He reached up a hand and brushed her cheek with his palm. Then he sighed. "I suppose you're sick of hearing how beautiful you are."

The non sequitur pulled her out of the dark place she'd been inhabiting for the last few minutes. She sniffled, and managed a small smile. "Depends on who's saying it."

"How about if I do?"

"Then it sounds wonderful."

One corner of his mouth lifted. "You'd better keep an eye on me, too."

"Why?"

"Because I want you like hell. I'll bet you hear that all the time, too."

She shook her head. "I've never heard that before."

"Amazing." He gave the slightest shake of his head. "I'd have thought guys would have been after you all the time."

"Not since Dean. Not even really before that. I didn't want it."

"Why not?"

She shrugged one shoulder, and let her cheek rest against his chest. She could hear the strong, steady beat of his heart, and the sound comforted her. "My dad left when I was little. I didn't know him. Mom managed, but it wasn't always easy for her. I made up my mind that I wanted to be independent, able to take care of myself, before I got knocked up."

"Knocked up?" The words came out on a surprised laugh.

"That's what happened to my mother. I grew up with plenty of cautions about letting hormones rule me, and making sure I didn't have kids until I found a man who would stick around. So I didn't even date much."

"No wonder you were such easy prey for Dean."

"You think?" She released a sigh, and with it the last of her tension.

"Well, that pretty much puts you off-limits," he said.

She looked up. "Why?"

"Because I wouldn't want to be the guy who put you on the trajectory for ruin."

"Would you really do that?"

He didn't even hesitate. "No. I couldn't live with myself."

"I didn't think so. Here you are willing to run off with me to protect me when you could just shrug it all off and agree that I should leave."

"No, I couldn't."

"Exactly." Her face still wet with tears, she continued to look into his eyes, and finally no matter how he argued with himself, he couldn't mistake the yearning he saw there. She wanted him, too. Maybe not as much or in the same way as he wanted her. Most likely she just needed the comfort of being needed.

If he had half a brain, he'd let her go now. But there were times when even half a brain wasn't enough.

"Kelly…"

"Kiss me?" she asked on the merest whisper. "Please? Just a kiss?"

"Are you sure?"

"Absolutely."

How could an ordinary cowboy argue with that? A kiss was a mere trifle. People kissed all the time. As long as it was just a kiss….

He lowered his head until their lips touched. The lightest of touches, just a shivery silky contact. She didn't recoil. In fact, he felt her lips part, felt her warm breath on his mouth. A shudder of raw longing ran through him. It had been too long, so achingly long since he had kissed a woman, and somehow Kelly wasn't just a woman to him. What she made him feel just then he was sure no one else could have made him feel.

That should have terrified him.

Instead, it warmed a cold place in his soul. Protectiveness surged in him along with yearning. Another fraction of an inch closer, and their lips met firmly. He couldn't have stopped then to save his life.

He deepened the kiss carefully, slowly, waiting on tenterhooks for any sign of rejection. None came. Her mouth moved gently against his, as if she were trying it out, too. Uncertain but hungry.

That hunger undid him. He ran his tongue over her lips until her mouth fell open to him, then he slipped his tongue into her warm moist depths, tasting her, letting her taste him.

Just a kiss. The understatement of his life.

His blood began to pound urgently, and he could feel himself hardening against her belly, an ache that had only one answer, an answer he couldn't take. Clinging to the last shred of his self-control, he went on kissing her, adjusting his hold on her to settle her more comfortably against him, letting her head fall back into the crook of his arm as he explored the gateway to passion.

When her arm lifted to encircle his neck, he almost lost it. He was experienced enough to know when a woman was totally open to him, and Kelly had just opened like a fresh rose. She wanted him every bit as much as he wanted her. There wasn't an ounce of resistance in her, only welcome.

Thunder seemed to pound in his head, but something else grew, too, a softening he hadn't ever felt before, a weakness like melting. It poured through him, like heat on a winter day, easing old aches. All he wanted to do was sink onto the floor with her and become a puddle.

He struggled for sense, even though every bit of him wanted to carry them both away to the ultimate intimacy.

It wasn't his sense that saved him. It was the doorbell.

"Oh!" Kelly gasped. An instant later she was standing a foot away, blinking as if she'd just awakened expectedly.

He recognized the look because he was feeling the same way. She looked at him with sleepy eyes that nonetheless contained astonishment.

Well, he was pretty astonished himself.

That had been one hell of a kiss.

The doorbell rang yet again, and he shook himself. "I'll get it. You stay out of sight."

Protecting her already. Well, he'd asked for it, and there was no way he was going to change his mind.

He opened the door and found Ben standing there looking concerned. The real estate agent wore the local costume of Western shirt, jeans, boots and cowboy hat, with the addition of a sports coat. It actually worked.

"What the hell is going on?" Ben demanded. "I got this

not-exactly-nice message on voice mail. Dammit, Hank, all I did was rent the place. That's what I'm supposed to do."

With a jerk of his head, Hank motioned him inside and closed the door. "What did you do? I told you this place wasn't ready to rent. The tenant and I have spent the last three days trying to make it safe for her."

"Oh, come on, you said the cutoffs on the stove were working. And you pulled the fuses on the bad circuits."

"But you didn't tell her there were problems. And you didn't warn her about the weak spots on the floor."

Ben flushed. "She's just renting for a couple of months. She didn't mind the condition of the place."

"She could have gotten hurt."

Ben's eyes widened, and Hank guessed that Kelly had come out of the bedroom. "Look," the agent said more reasonably, "I can give some of the money back."

"That's not the point," Hank said flatly. "I trusted you."

"It doesn't matter," Kelly said. "I'd have still rented it if I had known about the problems."

Hank looked over his shoulder at her. "You're not helping. I'm trying to take an inch out of his hide here."

Kelly surprised him with a giggle.

In spite of himself, Hank smiled. He loved to hear her laugh. But then he turned back to Ben who was relaxing. "I need to know something."

"What?"

"Did you do anything with the personal information Kelly gave you? A background check?"

"Of course I did! I had to check her credit rating."

Hank heard a thump behind him and turned to see that Kelly had sunk to the floor. That look of terror had come back to her face, and he had the worst urge to just punch Ben.

"It's normal procedure," Ben said, giving Kelly a quizzical look. "You don't just turn over property to people without making sure they're reasonably reliable. I'd have been delinquent in my job—"

Hank cut him off. "You've already been delinquent. You didn't do what I told you. Just get out of here. Now."

Ben didn't argue. Glaring at Hank, he turned and stomped out.

"Well," Hank said as he closed the door, "don't that just put the frosting on the cake."

He went to squat by Kelly, reaching for her hand. It was cold. "Lie down, Kelly. You've had a shock."

She didn't even argue. She slid down until she was on her back. He grabbed a nearby hassock to elevate her legs.

"Four days," she groaned. "Four days."

"I know." At that moment, the inside of his heart was as black as night.

"Four days," she said again, and again her tears started to roll.

There wasn't a damn thing he could do about it, either. Four days was long enough to track anyone down. If that guy was following her, if her husband wanted her dead, the killer could already be here.

"I'm calling the sheriff," he said. "You're going to be the best-protected person this side of the president."

She shook her head but didn't say anything. Nor could he really blame her. The sheriff didn't have enough people to surround her every minute. No way.

So that left him, a broken-down old cowboy.

Great. Just great.

Chapter 6

As the afternoon began to wane, Hank gave up on tearing up vinyl and linoleum. Through the open windows, he sensed the quickening of the breeze, and when he stepped outside, he saw storm clouds beginning to gather to the Southwest.

He went back in. "We're going to get rain. I need to finish caulking those windows now. Will you be okay if I'm right outside?"

He saw the flicker of hesitation, but it was brief. "Sure."

"I can be here in a split second. I'm not going anywhere." With effort, he squatted beside her and touched her shoulder with his fingertips. "Just promise me you won't decide to run without letting me know."

That eased her expression into a faint smile. "You want the truth? Now I'm afraid to run. Four days, Hank. That's long enough if he's hunting for me. He'd have known the instant my credit was queried."

"Yeah, I was afraid of that. He subscribes to one of those services?"

"Ever since somebody tried to use his identity to buy a car."

"Hell." He moved until he gripped her shoulder. "One peep from you and I'll be in here faster than you can say squat. I promise. But I had to put in wood-frame windows because someone twenty years back decided we needed to preserve our historical heritage. I don't need to tell you the frames will swell if I don't get the caulking done."

Her smile widened a shade. "You don't like historic preservation?"

"Depends. I tried to talk 'em into letting me use vinyl frames that look the same, but no dice. Some people are idiots. Vinyl at least doesn't change its size with every change in humidity."

She nodded. "I don't know much about it."

"I do. Sticky windows are going to be unavoidable over time. On the other hand, I was able to plane the frames for a perfect fit. Couldn't have done that with metal or vinyl."

A dagger sliced through his hip and he had to stand up. "I just need to run next door to get my caulking gear. Wanna come?"

Again that fleeting hesitation. Then a look of determination. "No, I'll just keep pulling up the flooring. It's such a mess now I just want to get it done."

"Sorry I can't get it out of here until they get the big trash container out here tomorrow."

"It's not a big deal. It's just that I'm starting to see progress. It makes me want to keep going."

He looked around and had to agree. They'd definitely made a lot of progress. Sadly, the wood under the vinyl flooring was covered with glue. That was going to take a real cleaning job.

"Okay. I'll be back in five. As soon as I get the caulking done, we're going to get some dinner. Sound good?"

"Sounds great."

It was only as he limped as quickly as he could over to his place that he realized he didn't want to leave her alone for even five minutes. Not since that little conversation with Ben a few hours ago.

As irritated as he was with Ben for renting the place in that condition, he couldn't get irritated with him for doing a background check on Kelly. Under any other circumstances, it was what he would have expected of Ben. The man had just been doing his job.

And he couldn't have known it might put Kelly at risk.

That it probably had.

Oh, Hank did not like the storm of feelings that had been battering at the edges of his mind all afternoon. Between them, he and Ben may have set a trap for her, with the best intentions in the world. He, with his inquiry to the police because he wanted to know what was really going on; Ben with his principled conduct of his job.

Didn't make it feel any better. The thunder that rumbled out of the Southwest echoed the rumbling in his mind. A storm was brewing, all right, and he'd helped make it.

Although in honesty, he hadn't meant it to. He hadn't thought a quiet inquiry to the police might get back to anyone outside the department. But, sadly, Kelly was right. If Dean was playing the distraught soon-to-be-ex concerned about his wife's disappearance, if he had reported her missing—and he might well have to try to cover himself since she had already been attacked once—then some kind soul at the police department, if he heard about the request for information from Denver, would undoubtedly have let Dean know that she had surfaced.

That alone wouldn't do much. No, it was the confluence of things that might now create a serious risk for her. Her being ID'd in Laramie before the query from Denver could have sent Dean and his compadre looking in the wrong direction, but a credit check out of Conard County, Wyoming nailed her whereabouts. Cripes, they might as well have handed over her address.

He grabbed his caulk and caulking gun and hurried back to the house as swiftly as he could. He was relieved to see Kelly still ripping at the floor, ripping as if her life depended on it.

She had to be terrified. The amazing thing to him was how little she showed it. It was as if she were a cork, wanting to bob up no matter how many times she got shoved down. He liked that.

"I'm back," he said.

She looked over her shoulder, then sat back on her heels, pushing strands of blond hair back from her face. "I know. You have a distinctive walk."

"You mean I hobble. Hard to mistake."

The corners of her mouth lifted upward. "What happened?"

"Another time," he said, swiftly evading the subject that caused him so much pain. Hell, he apparently wasn't half as brave as she was. He waved his caulking gear at her. "This has to come first. That storm is moving in fast."

She hesitated. "Can we close the windows?"

She asked with studied casualness, but he saw past it. "Sure. And lock the doors, too, if you want. I'm just going to be right outside."

"Won't the rain damage the caulking?"

"Nah. I buy the good stuff. It'll be set up well enough in half an hour, and it won't rain before then."

Outside, though, he took another look at the sky. Yeah, there was time. For this at any rate. The rest he wasn't so sure about.

Kelly pulled up the last of the kitchen flooring and carried it over to add it to the building heap in the living room. Her arms ached, her back ached and she thanked God for the hard physical labor, because without it she'd be crawling out of her skin with nerves.

How often did Dean get those reports from the credit bureaus? Every day? Only when there was activity? Would a credit check alone send him an immediate alert?

She ought to know these things, but there was a lot she didn't know because Dean had controlled everything.

A gilded cage. Another platitude. Man, the entire past eight years were turning into one big, ugly trite platitude. And she wasn't happy about it.

Standing here now at the age of twenty-nine, she could look back and shake her head over her own blindness. And wonder how she could have been so consistently blind.

How had she done it? How was it possible not to see what was right under your nose? Anyone with half a brain would have wondered what Dean saw in her. Anyone with half a brain would have thought it was a mismatch that simply wouldn't work because of the age difference, if nothing else.

He was a man of the world. He'd been around almost every corner. Why hadn't she wondered what about her could possibly attract him? Why hadn't she once questioned his declaration of love?

Looking back at their early dates, she sagged into a kitchen chair with a glass of water, and tried to remember what they'd talked about. And, looking back, she remembered that he'd done most of the talking while she hung on every word. He spun fabulous travelogues of all the exotic places he had visited and wanted to take her. They'd even managed to visit a few of them, always in the company of other friends, though.

Maybe that should have been a clue. They went to Venice, they went to Dublin, they went to London. But never just the two of them. No, they always travelled with Dean's friends, and she'd spent her share of time sitting in cafés with the other wives, or reading books waiting for him to get back from some excursion that was just for the "guys."

Other times they'd done everything as a group. But never, ever, had Dean seemed the least bit interested in sneaking away with her. Not even their so-called honeymoon had been just the two of them.

She closed her eyes against a sudden shaft of pain, facing anew the fact that she had been used from the very beginning. There had never been a honeymoon, not in that marriage. Never a time when she had felt that Dean was focused solely on her. Except possibly in bed, and then only when it was new.

How could she have failed to notice that? Simply because she didn't have experience? Shouldn't there at least have been a few early days when Dean had devoted himself to her?

Or was that hindsight speaking again? Maybe some people never fell in love that way, so intensely that they could think of little else. She had, but that didn't mean Dean was that type. He was older, after all, maybe past that rush of new love. Maybe that was just a youthful thing.

Or maybe she was still trying to make excuses for him. Still trying to believe that he hadn't married her just because she'd look good on his arm and make other men envious.

A tap startled her. Her eyes flew open and she saw Hank outside the window with his caulking gun. He smiled, gave her a little wave, then started running a bead of caulk around the frame.

She wondered if Hank would be the type to fall in love the way she had, where the whole world went away in the wonder of it. If he would see the sun rise and set in someone's eyes the way she had once seen it in Dean's. The thought made her catch her breath, and her heart skipped a few beats. What a thought!

It was enough to make her sit straighter in her chair, to quicken her breath and awaken an ache between her thighs.

To be loved by someone the way she had once loved Dean. To be loved that way by a man like Hank, who seemed so down-to-earth and kind.

Even as emotionally bruised as she felt, she couldn't help but envy the woman Hank would someday love. Something about him suggested that he would be a devoted mate. Although maybe she would be smarter to assume she was no judge of such things.

Dean was proof positive of that.

Hank disappeared from the kitchen windows and came into the house through the mudroom. Since their reinforcement of the joists, the floor no longer creaked under his weight.

"Almost done," he said. "That storm's getting closer. You want to spend the night at my place? I've got that spare room."

Her heart nearly stopped. But he'd said *spare room*. "Why? Is it going to be bad?"

"It looks like it. But it's not just the storm. I looked through the kitchen window and…you looked so sad. Plus, I've been stewing all afternoon, and I don't think you should be alone. So either you take my spare room tonight, or I'm sleeping here on the floor."

She couldn't help it. She looked around. "What floor?"

A crack of laughter escaped him. "That's a good question."

The sound of his laugh brightened her mood a bit. "I guess you leave me no choice."

"That was the plan."

She looked at him, wondering how it was she had stumbled on a knight errant at the point in her life when she most needed one. Maybe the Fates weren't entirely without compassion. "Thanks, Hank. The spare room it is."

She'd hardly unpacked. In fact, she hadn't really unpacked in over six weeks, except to do laundry as necessary. Easy, therefore, to pack an overnight bag. Heck, it wasn't as if she had much at all.

Hank looked at her duffel as she flung it over her shoulder. "Is that all you left with?"

"A duffel? Yes. I had to be able to carry it easily."

"Hell," he said quietly. "I could get really, really angry about now."

"It's fine," she said quickly. "It's enough. I don't need much."

"Few of us do, I suppose." He shook his head. "If you have laundry you want to bring, you can use my machines."

So she gathered up her dirty clothing in a canvas bag she carried for that purpose and brought it along. Outside, the sky had become overcast, though the darkest clouds still remained a distance away. For the first time, she heard the low growl of distant thunder.

She had certainly been preoccupied, she thought, because she hadn't even noticed either the darkening or the rumbling until just now. The air had cooled noticeably, and she shivered.

"I'm Florida-born-and-bred," she said as they climbed his porch steps. "I'll have to get a jacket if I'm going to be here long."

"We get plenty hot sometimes, but I have to admit most

of the time around here it would probably feel cool to you. I have a zippered hoodie you're welcome to borrow."

"I think I'll take you up on it. I've been thinking as I got further north that I'd need something, but I was never anywhere long enough to do something about it."

"But you get cold down there, too, don't you?"

"Of course. But your summertime temperatures are reminding me of my wintertime temperatures."

He flashed her a smile as he let her into his house. "At least now you're out of the wind. Let me get you that sweatshirt."

He dropped her duffel and laundry in a room down the hall as he headed back through the house. Two minutes later he emerged from a room and handed her a navy blue hoodie. "Sorry, it's the only clean one I have that isn't ragged."

She shook out the folds and found herself staring at a shirt with a quatrefoil shield on it, like a four-leaf clover, and the letters DFD, only a large Gothic *D* overlaid the *FD*. She held it, looking at him, feeling that something very sensitive might be happening.

"Are you sure you want me to wear this?" For days now, any time the subject came up he had said so firmly that he was just a cowboy now. She was certain this shirt had associations he didn't like to think about.

"It's not a problem," he said, shrugging one shoulder. "You need to be warm. That'll work better than anything else I have." As if to prove it meant nothing, he took it from her, unzipped it and helped slip it around her shoulders. It was huge, but it was also soft and warm, and she hugged it around herself.

"Thanks, this feels so good."

"I thought it might. Feel free to roll up the sleeves."

He passed her, heading for the kitchen. "Are you hungry? Because I'm sure getting there."

"Ravenous," she admitted, following him. "What can I do to help?"

"Just take a seat and keep me company."

Thunder boomed loudly and the lights flickered briefly, as if the storm wanted to make sure it had their attention.

"I guess it's good I have a gas stove," he remarked as he opened the refrigerator and began pulling things out. Then he volunteered something about himself for the first time. "I'm not a bad cook."

"You make great tuna salad and grilled cheese sandwiches."

"I make more than that. When you live at the firehouse, you take turns cooking for everyone. You'd better be passable or you'll be working with a lot of unhappy guys."

"You do that for yourselves?"

"One of the guys was designated cook, another a designated shopper." He paused, his hands full of fresh vegetables. "But basically, we can all fill in when needed. You don't suppose they're going to hire cooks and cleaners for us, do you?"

"But cops don't have to."

"They don't work our shifts. Besides, it's an old tradition. As old as the first volunteer fire department, I guess." He placed the vegetables on the counter and stuck his head back in the fridge. "They liked my cooking. So I did a lot of it when I had the time."

"Was that often?"

"Depends." This time he emerged with what appeared to be a package of chops and placed it near the vegetables. "The average fire takes a couple of hours to deal with. We have to clean all the equipment, too, to make sure it's operational and ready for the next call. And then there are other emergencies. So, no, there isn't a whole lot of free time, but there's some. We schedule training days and cleaning days, and in between we cook, sleep and shoot the breeze. Anyway, it's flexible. It's not like I don't answer a call because someone has to cook. There are older guys who often stay behind."

She noticed that he didn't use the past tense. So part of him was still on that job, still a fireman. "I couldn't imagine being a firefighter. Fire terrifies me."

"It terrifies most people. Me included."

"Then how do you do it?"

"It's an essential job. Some of us can swallow the fear enough to do it. Some of us even get a kick out of it."

"Did you?"

He shook his head. "I'm not an adrenaline junky. I used up a lifetime's worth of adrenaline on that job."

"Then what drew you to it?"

"I…wanted to be useful. Save lives. Do something I could be proud of."

"I wish I'd done just one thing in my life that important."

"You will. Important things don't always have a lot of flash, but they're still important." He gave her a reassuring smile and turned to start unwrapping the vegetables.

"I still can't imagine it," she said after a few moments. "I don't think I could go into a burning building for anything."

"You'd be surprised how many people do just that because someone they love is still inside. Or maybe a pet."

"So many? I mean I've heard about it, but I thought it wasn't very many people who did that."

"I lost count of the times we had to hold someone back. People lose their fear sometimes, most especially when someone they love is at risk."

"I guess. But what's your excuse?"

At that, a crack of laughter escaped him. "Haven't you heard the old joke? Firefighters are the stupidest people on earth. When everyone else is running out of a burning building, we're running in."

That got a small laugh from her, even as she shook her head. "You're not stupid at all."

"No," he agreed. He leaned back against the counter, his face tight, and the way he stood suggested to her that he was hurting again and needed a brief break. "No, we're not stupid. But I do think we're built differently. We're missing the survival gene or something. I don't know. I just know not everyone can do it, and those of us who do don't really think about what we're doing when we're doing it. We rely on training, experience and intuition, and there's just no room for fear after that first step."

He sighed and ran his fingers through his shaggy hair. "I don't know how to explain it exactly, Kelly. It's like being a cop. You couldn't pay me to do that job."

She nodded, but didn't ask any more questions, wanting him to talk at his own pace. And no matter how he minimized it, her awe of him was growing.

"I knew a reporter who could have been a firefighter," he said after a moment. "That gal was a pistol. She'd hear the call come in and the next thing we knew she'd be in her car riding our bumper right through stoplights."

"Now that's crazy."

He chuckled. "I don't think so. She wanted that story the way we wanted to put out that fire. She even volunteered to go into our training room with us and see what it was like in full gear when the temperatures hit the roof. Gotta give her credit for that, even if we did have to drag her out. The heat weakened her and she wasn't used to the weight of the equipment. But man, she had fun."

Kelly tried to imagine it. "I'm not sure I could do that, even as part of training."

"I think you could," he said firmly. "Quit putting yourself down. Anyway, she gave one of our captains a conniption."

"How'd she do that?"

"We'd been called out to help with a forest fire just outside of town. Big one. So we're pushing into the fire and coming back out after a specified period of time, working to keep it from jumping a road. And she remarked on the fact that we couldn't get enough of the smoke. Captain asked her why and she said, 'Because the first thing all you guys do when you pull off your masks is light a cigarette.'"

At that Kelly laughed.

"But then," Hank continued, "she pointed at the ground around the captain's feet. The butts must have been an inch deep."

Kelly laughed even harder. "That's so funny. But why did it bother the captain?"

"Because the chief didn't want us to be caught smoking in some newspaper photo. Bad for the image."

Kelly giggled. "Do you smoke?"

"I did back then. I quit a while ago."

And she could almost see the door slam down, the drawbridge go up, whatever. He'd said all he wanted to say, at least for now. She'd learned from Dean that ignoring such hints could only lead to trouble, and her laughter died.

Hank sighed, as if he sensed that he'd upset her somehow. "I was trying to make you laugh," he said.

"I know. It was funny."

"Good." Then he turned his back and started washing vegetables and slicing them with a big chef's knife on a cutting board.

"So you liked this reporter?"

"We all did. Great sense of humor, and I think she was as crazy as we were."

"I can't imagine you crazy."

A snort escaped him. "Everyone is capable of some craziness. No, I just meant that her job gave her the same kind of sense of black humor as we had."

"The cat in the tree thing?"

"Yeah, like that." But even looking at his backside, she could tell that he had tensed again. What about cats could make him stiffen like that? All she could do was wonder.

All of a sudden he put down the knife and hobbled over to sit across from her at the table. "I'm sorry," he said.

"For what?"

"I keep shutting you out. In some ways I'm a walking minefield. But you've been open with me, so I guess I should give you the same."

"You don't have to."

"Yes, I do. Right now you're trusting me. I'm sure you'd feel a whole lot better about that if I didn't just suddenly clam up on you. I know I do that. And I know it makes people uneasy."

"Hank, you don't…"

But he interrupted her. "It's a simple story. Two years ago I went into a burning building because we had a report there was a woman in there. I knew I was putting my neck on the line. The fire was bad, and the building was no longer structurally sound. But I couldn't leave someone in there, so I went. And with me went two of my best friends, Allan Kurst and Fran Beacham. The place collapsed on us. I was the only one who survived, and I was pretty well smashed up."

Kelly listened speechlessly, her heart squeezing with pain for him.

"Fran took the brunt, I guess. I hear she was draped over me when they found me. Anyway, it turned out the woman we were trying to rescue had already managed to get out, but none of her friends knew it. So it was stupid, useless and reckless, and I lost my best friend and the woman I was getting ready to ask to marry me. End of story."

Somehow she doubted that was anywhere near the end of the story. His gray eyes reflected pain and loss, and undoubtedly the physical pain and limp he still suffered from were the result of being crushed under that building.

"I was lucky," he said. "Do you have any idea how tired I am of hearing I was lucky?"

"Maybe."

His eyes widened a shade, and the pain vanished in a short, unexpected laugh. "Maybe you do," he said. "Maybe you do."

Chapter 7

The washing machine rumbled in the background along with thunder as they ate a meal of marinated pork chops, salad and seasoned brown rice.

They had been quiet ever since Hank had told her his story, and Kelly felt awkward. He'd made it sound so straightforward, but she hadn't missed the part about losing the woman he wanted to marry and his best friend at the same time. And, equally bad, their act of bravery, the losses, had all turned out to be unnecessary.

She couldn't imagine living with that. But maybe he couldn't imagine living with a killer on his heels. If she hadn't fought her attacker off, it never would have been real for her. She might have died without ever believing that Dean was capable of such a thing.

But her entire worldview had changed in the wee hours of one morning when she stood in the muck and the reeds, dizzy from a blow to the head, fighting like a maniac for survival. Nothing would ever be the same again.

Hank must feel like that. The shock of what had happened must still be rippling through his life. It was probably the reason he kept insisting that he was just a cowboy. Because he didn't want to be constantly reminded.

As if his limp and what appeared to be unending pain didn't remind him every time he moved.

How did you live with that?

She wanted to ask, but again hesitated. He'd opened up, but maybe he'd said all he could on the subject. Much as she wanted to know how he coped, she didn't want to wound him by asking.

For the first time in months, Kelly found herself worrying about someone besides herself. It was a momentous internal shift, and she looked down at her plate, feeling ashamed of how self-absorbed she had become.

It was understandable enough since she was attacked, but before that? She'd been drowning in self-pity and anger when she was facing nothing that hundreds of thousands of other women didn't face: a marriage gone bad. Oh, and the loss of so-called friends, most of whom probably felt threatened because she, alone among them, had decided to step out of her gilded cage.

Yes, she'd been feeling pretty sorry for herself, and, thinking about it now, she squirmed a bit in her chair.

"Something wrong?"

Hank's calm, deep voice drew her back to the present.

"Not really. I was just thinking how much I've been feeling sorry for myself."

"You have cause."

"Do I really? Yes, I had a marriage that didn't work. Whatever the reasons for it, that's not exactly noteworthy. I decided to leave because he had started to hit me. A lot of women don't get that choice, or if they do they can't make it because they have kids to worry about, or no way to support themselves, or maybe they're too terrified to leave. I left. That put me ahead of the game, not behind. But I was oh-so-sorry for myself. And then I felt even sorrier for myself when my friends told me I was being stupid and pretty much stopped talking to me."

"They did that?"

"Yes. Some friends."

"Exactly." He put his knife and fork down and gave her his full attention. "Small loss, apparently."

"Apparently. But that didn't keep me from feeling wronged and deserted. So I stumbled along for most of a year holding a royal pity party, at least when I wasn't so angry at Dean that I wanted my lawyer to make him hurt where it counts—in his wallet. It was ugly, Hank. *I* was ugly."

"I think you were probably just reacting normally." He reached across the table and covered her fisted hand with his big one. Calluses, rough skin, warmth. She liked the way his hand felt. "Divorce can't be easy, no matter why it happens."

"It's not," she agreed. "The first thing that hit me was I felt like such a failure because I couldn't make it work. I mean, I'm one of those types who actually thinks marriage is forever."

"I am, too," he said. "Unfortunately, it isn't always. You didn't know what kind of man Dean would turn out to be."

"No, I didn't. But I still felt like a failure. The only reason I didn't leave the first time he hit me was because I was sure I must have done something to deserve it, sure he wouldn't do it again, and positive that if I just tried harder, things would get better."

"I'd think that's pretty normal."

"Maybe. And I didn't want my marriage to fail. I mean,

that's what divorce is—a failure. Maybe you've done everything you can, maybe you haven't, but something gets broken, and it's a failure."

"That's a pretty strong word."

"What else would you call it?" She sighed, realizing that her chest was growing tight with a whole welter of emotions she could barely sort out. "One of us failed or both of us failed—what difference does it make? It meant admitting I'd been wrong about a lot of things. Facing the fact that I'd made a poor judgment. That *for better or for worse* wasn't a touchstone I could live by."

"Hey," he said quietly, squeezing her hand. "I don't think that phrase was meant to apply to abuse."

"In the past it was."

He sighed, squeezed her hand again and let go, leaning back in his chair. "That was then. We've since come to the conclusion that no one should have to endure being beaten by a spouse. That it's as much a crime as if a stranger did it. We do occasionally evolve."

The way he said it eased some of the tightness in her chest. "I guess." She drew a deep breath, trying to let go of the strangling feelings. They eased, but only a bit. "I bounced back and forth a lot about it. Sometimes I hated myself. Sometimes I hated him. I guess some part of me will always wonder if I could have done something different and changed things."

"I know that feeling."

His tone yanked her out of her self-absorption. His face had once again tightened, and she wanted to kick herself for the inadvertent reminder of what he'd been through. "I'm sorry. I shouldn't have said that."

"Why not? It's true. I've been second-guessing myself for two years now. You know what? It doesn't change a damn thing. Because no matter how much I question myself I always get the same answer. Believing there was a woman trapped in that building, I would still go into it."

She nodded, and now she reached for his hand, to cover it with hers and hold on tightly. "You would have. I can tell. Unless you had some way of knowing something different, you wouldn't change your decision."

"Well, the same goes for you," he said a trifle harshly. "You were young and in love. The information you had at the time didn't warn you, did it?"

She hesitated, bit her lip and shook her head. "No."

"Then stop it. Stop wondering if you could have changed anything. If there's one thing I know for sure, that's the path to insanity."

He rose from the table without another word, and limped quickly from the kitchen.

Kelly felt about two inches tall. Her problems seemed so petty next to what had happened to him. Well, the ones she had been talking about, anyway. The idea that Dean wanted her dead still loomed pretty large on any scale, but the rest of it?

Damn! She tossed her napkin on the table and rose, not at all sure what she was going to do, or if she could do anything. By falling back into self-pity mode, she'd opened a can of worms for Hank. She wished she could bite her tongue off.

But it was too late now.

Hank stood at the front bay window, watching the trees toss in the storm, listening to the rattle of large raindrops against the windowpane and the increasingly loud booms of thunder.

His hips were screaming at him, his back was hammering a painful tattoo and even his knees seemed angry at him. A bitter thought drifted to the foreground, bitterness about his current condition. He'd just promised a woman he would protect her, but if he were to be honest, he couldn't be sure he was physically capable of doing that anymore. The guy who had run into fires to save lives could no longer run across his own lawn with any confidence.

Some hero. She was looking to him as if he were a lifesaver, sharing things with him she had shared with no one else, trusting him to keep her safe.

Two years ago he could have been reasonably certain he could do that. Today he had no right to invite anyone to rely on his protection because, dammit, his body was no longer the reliable machine it had once been. He hated that. He hated that almost as much as he hated having lost Fran and Allan.

And second-guessing. Hell, he'd done enough of that himself. He supposed he should have been more understanding of what Kelly was saying, but he knew that road she was walking and it didn't do a damn bit of good.

Once he had made peace with the fact that he would have gone into that building all over again under the same circumstances, he'd had to make peace with the rest of it. She needed to do the same.

"Hank? I'm sorry."

"Don't apologize." He heard her come up beside him, but he wasn't ready to look at her. Not yet. Not when he felt like such a sham himself.

But then he felt her arm steal around his waist and give him a hug. He almost held his breath, hoping she didn't pull away, as a huge rush of warmth ran through him.

She didn't pull away. He closed his eyes a moment, amazed at the trust she was showing him after all she'd been through. Maybe she'd moved on better than she realized.

"You're right about second-guessing," she said after a few minutes. "Absolutely right."

"We do it anyway."

"But after a certain point, it's a waste of time and energy, isn't it? Because once you've learned what there is to learn, you should let it go."

Feeling oddly awkward, he slipped his own arm around her shoulders. It had been way too long since he'd embraced a woman this way, with a feeling of companionship. And it felt so damn good. The idea that he had no right to her trust seemed to be slipping away on a tide of need.

"Letting go isn't always easy," he admitted. "And I had plenty of psychological help afterward. Unfortunately, we can't go back and change our decisions. Sometimes if we're honest with ourselves about what we knew when we made them, we know we'd do it all over again."

"Yeah."

Was he mistaken, or did she edge a tiny bit closer? His heart tripped. God, he didn't want to take advantage of her, but he knew his own growing weakness: He wanted her. A whole helluva lot.

"I guess," she said after a moment, "that that's the hard part. Accepting that we can't change it, because later it all looks so…so…"

"Inconceivable?" he suggested. "Because I'm not going to say stupid. I fought that battle once already, and there's no point in your fighting it. If I've managed to learn one thing out of the mess I went through, it's that you have to cut yourself some slack. Nobody's perfect, nobody's omniscient and we're all just muddling through the best we can."

A short laugh escaped her. "Dean never muddles."

"No?"

"Not to hear him tell it, anyway."

"Well, he seems to have muddled with you a bit."

"How so?"

The wind kicked up outside, and Hank didn't speak for a few moments as he watched a tree bend, waiting for it to crack or get uprooted. It didn't. And then the drum of rain on the roof became almost deafening.

He turned from the window, his arm still around Kelly's shoulders. "He muddled," he said firmly. "He didn't realize what a prize he had in you."

"I'm no prize."

"But you were. Young, beautiful, devoted, bright and so very much in love with him. He should have cherished you, not trampled on you."

He watched her blink in surprise, saw the astonishment in her blue eyes, on her face. "I don't think…"

"No, don't argue. You gave him one of life's most precious gifts—the true, pure, first love of a young woman."

He watched color rise in her cheeks, visible even though the day had darkened almost to smudge. "I mean that," he said.

He could see her thinking about that. "You know, you sound almost medieval."

"What do you mean?"

One corner of her mouth lifted. "You're a knight errant. You believe in romantic love. Chivalry."

For an instant the blackness almost seized him again, that acute awareness of his physical shortcomings. Knight errant? Not likely. But the gloom that tried to creep in lost out to the ridiculous image of himself in armor and carrying a lance. In spite of himself, he grinned. "No, my lady, that's a pedestal too high for me. I'm just a cowboy. A crippled one at that."

But even as she grinned back at him, he saw another thought occur to her, and her smile faded. "Hank?"

"Yes?"

"Are you saying what I have to offer now isn't as good?"

Oh, man. The question pierced him and he gripped her by the shoulders. He shook his head, irritated with himself.

"All I meant was that Dean was a fool for not realizing what a prize you were. Not that you aren't still a prize."

At that, some of the doubt left her and she smiled almost shyly. "Keep talking, cowboy. My ego could use a boost."

"I suppose it could." Given what she'd been through, a huge boost might be in order. The problem was that he had no idea how to provide it, or even if he could.

All he could think to do, however, was pull her close for a hug as the storm raged outside. Inside, however, it was as if the storm went away. Inside, he felt things he hadn't felt in a long time—how good it was to hold a woman close. Just how damn good a hug felt. So good.

He tipped his head a bit, pressing his face into her hair, and inhaling deeply. He could smell the faint aroma of a perfumed shampoo, mixed with the scents of woman, of a woman who had worked hard that day. He felt intoxicated by it.

"With Fran," he said huskily, "it was different," he said simply. For some reason, he needed her to know that. He didn't know what it was yet—it might be nothing at all—but it was just different. And that was good.

"Good," she said, almost as if she read his mind. She lifted her other arm so that she hugged him back with both. "It's different for me, too."

"Good."

She snuggled closer, and the warmth grew in him, like a morning sun rising, burning off the chill of a long, cold night. Such feelings were dangerous, but just then he didn't care. It had been so long since he'd felt that kind of internal warmth, that kind of easing of every tension and bad memory. Peace, that's what it was, as if all the burdens had been lifted.

And by something as simple as a hug.

Without thinking, he kissed her on the head. But at that moment his hip chose to stab him with a pain so sharp he stumbled.

"Hank? Hank, are you all right?"

The pang was so severe he couldn't even answer. He dragged himself over to the couch and flopped, coming down mostly on his back, grabbing his knee and trying to stretch out the hip joint.

Kelly flew to his side, kneeling beside him. "What can I do?" she asked desperately.

"Wait." It was all he could squeeze out. It would pass, the worst of it. It always did. But damn, he hated when it came out of the blue like this, without even a warning so he could get ready. And he thought he was going to protect her?

She continued to kneel beside him, and every time he opened his eyes, he saw her worry. "It'll pass," he managed. "It'll pass."

And finally it began to ease, as if the daggers that had been thrust into him were being removed one by one. Slowly, cautiously, he stretched his leg out.

"Damn!" He swore quietly but emphatically.

"Are you okay?" she asked. Her face pinched with concern.

"Yeah. Yeah. I'm fine. Just don't ever let anyone tell you that being crushed under a three-story building can be fully repaired."

Her lips pursed. Then a crooked smile appeared. "You get around pretty well, for a lame cowboy."

He drew a couple of deep breaths, trying to summon an answering smile for her. "Yeah, reckon I do."

Her brow knit. "How bad was it?"

"Bad," he admitted. He tried to sit up, but his hip voiced an opinion about that, so he let himself fall back.

"What? A hip? More than that?"

"A lot more. One hip had to be replaced. And given the trouble I have with the one they repaired, sometimes I think about having it replaced, too. Fractured pelvis. Broken ribs, broken legs…aw, hell, Kelly, I was basically raspberry gelatin in a skin pouch."

She winced and grimaced. "My God."

"Well, that's how the doc described it. Although I don't think it was quite *that* bad."

"And burns? Did you get burned, too?"

"Some, but not a whole lot. Most of it was on my back. Medically induced comas are wonderful things."

"I can imagine."

"No damage to my spine, although the muscles got pretty insulted by the impact with my breathing tank. So, see, I *was* lucky."

She sat back on her heels, just looking at him. "*Lucky*. I'm starting to hate that word."

"I've felt that way myself, from time to time."

"You must have been in the hospital forever."

"Actually, only a couple of months. Then I was in rehab, because I had to learn to walk with all the new parts. But I get around pretty well now."

"You sure do. But you hurt all the time, don't you?"

"Well, some. Most of the time I can ignore it. Sometimes, like just now, not so much."

So there, he'd told her he was a busted-up husk of a man, and by rights she should be looking for someone else to watch over her, because at this moment he doubted he'd be much help if the bad guys showed up. Of course, that was *this* moment.

But she amazed him. Instead of getting all distressed because he'd helped draw a killer her way, and then had offered protection he might well not be capable of providing, she leaned forward and kissed his cheek. Her lips were warm, the touch like fire. It zinged through his body, making things ache in a totally different way.

"You're a hero, Hank Jackson."

"Aw, hell, don't say that!" She couldn't have chosen better words to make him angry. And anger was enough to make it possible for him to sit up.

"Why not?"

"I'm no hero. Because I went back into that building, two of the people I loved most in the world followed me. They wouldn't let me go alone. And they died. *They're* the heroes."

She had sat back on her heels again, and her face expressed distress, and maybe even a little anger of her own. "Maybe you don't think so," she said quietly.

"Not only don't I think so, I never want to hear that freaking word again! God, I wish they hadn't followed me. I made the decision, I should be the one taking a dirt nap. Instead, my best friends are dead."

Thunder boomed so loudly the house shook, but neither of them moved. Hank was panting with anger and pain, and Kelly was looking up at him with wide blue eyes that revealed nothing.

"I think," she said, "that you misunderstood me. I meant you're a hero now. A lot of people couldn't live with the kind of pain you're experiencing."

"A lot of people do," he grumped. But his anger began to ease.

"How much pain medication do you take?"

The question caught him unawares. "Why? Just some aspirin."

"Yeah, I didn't think you looked like you take something like oxycontin."

"I did for a while."

"I'm sure. But I've seen plenty of Dean's patients, none of whom went through anything like what you go through every day, begging for more pain relief. Dean used to talk about it. Women who should have been far enough past surgery to settle for aspirin or a little codeine whined that they couldn't stand the pain."

"Did he give them what they wanted?"

She shrugged. "Probably. Dean wanted happy patients."

"Some people don't handle pain very well."

"Trust me, they never suffered what you suffered. And they'd be back for more in a couple of years, so it couldn't have been *that* bad. But you, you'd be justified in being on something stronger, at least some of the time, and you settle for aspirin. In my book, that makes you a hero."

And for once the word didn't tighten his stomach into an iron knot. But he still dismissed it. "I'm no hero. We all do what we have to in life. That doesn't make us heroes."

"Maybe not."

He was grateful that she didn't argue further, but he had to admit that she had just put a new spin on the word *hero* for him. Maybe it wasn't so bad after all. The world was full of heroes of the type she was talking about. He'd met more than a handful in rehab, or those times when the department would visit the children's cancer ward.

The worst of the pain in his hip eased, and he leaned back, ignoring the sensation of grinding glass. Kelly stood, shaking out her legs, and came to sit beside him. The room was even darker now, as evening added to the storm's blackness.

Another boom of thunder shook the house, and lightning flashed blindingly.

Hank reached out, felt for her hand and took it. He had avoided the contact of touch for a long time now, until Kelly in fact. And only in the last couple of days, since she had come into his life, did he realize how much he had missed it.

Gratitude filled him as she turned her hand over and clasped his. "This is some storm," she remarked. "Like the ones we get in Miami. Maybe worse, except for tropical storms and hurricanes."

"They can get pretty strong here," he agreed. "At least we don't get a lot of tornadoes."

Lightning flared again, blinding him, followed by another boom that shook the house.

"The mountains," he volunteered, "usually block the worst weather from getting to us. It has to come up from the south, this kind of weather."

"You studied meteorology?"

He shook his head, smiling faintly. "No, just some stuff I picked up along the way." Then he asked a question. "The way you were talking about Dean's patients, it sounds like you don't exactly approve of plastic surgery."

A few seconds passed before she answered. "I don't *dis*approve. I understand that some people's self-image and prospects are totally tied up with how they look. And plastic surgeons work miracles for people with all kinds of burns and other serious defects."

"But the way you talked about those women…" He let the thought dangle.

"Well," she said frankly, "I think some of them would do better to spend their money on a therapist. Every surgery is dangerous. Things can go wrong. Infections happen. It's not something to do lightly. But some of them did it just that way."

"I see."

Another flare of lightning allowed him to see her shake her head as she continued speaking. "And some of them couldn't understand, no matter how often Dean explained, that there's a limit to the number of face-lifts you can have without looking like a wax doll. Just so much he can tighten skin, and just so often. So eventually, age takes its toll. There's no permanent escape. All you can do is delay it."

"I didn't know that."

"It's true. It always amazed me how young some of our patients were, too. They'd start pushing twenty-five and they'd already be looking for botox or other procedures."

She turned a little on the couch so that she was looking at him. As dark as it was, he doubted that she could see much, and he wondered if he should turn on a light. But she didn't ask, and he was enjoying the darkness.

She continued speaking. "I think that's sick, even if I did win the looks lottery. Besides, what good did it do me to be beautiful? I wasted eight years of my life with a man who would never have noticed me if my nose were too big."

"Ouch."

"It's the truth."

"Let me tell you something. Truth." He held his hand up as if taking an oath. "I'm a man like any other, but I generally don't think about how people look. Most look pretty good actually, especially when they're feeling good and they smile. Fran used to complain that her shoulders were too broad, that her face was too round, that she had an overlapping tooth she wished she could have fixed. I never noticed those things. I thought she was perfect."

"I'm sure she was." Kelly sighed, then surprised him by touching his cheek briefly. "I'm sorry about Fran."

"Me, too. She was a great friend, a great partner. I'll always miss her." With effort he shook off the mood that was in danger of descending on him. "But I can't change it. I took up a lot of therapy time with that one."

"I can imagine. I'd probably do the same, but with a lot less reason."

"Don't minimize what you went through. That doesn't help anything. We both lost love, just in different ways."

She surprised him then by curling into his side and resting her head on his shoulder. "Is this okay?"

It was more than okay. He liked it. Moving gingerly, he put his arm around her. "It's fine."

"I'm starting to doubt myself again," she said quietly.

"About what?"

"About whether that guy who attacked me was sent by Dean. Maybe it *was* just a random attack."

"A rather strange one. I guess if he's after you, we're going to find out. If not, well, I'll go with you to Miami for your court date."

She sighed and snuggled a little closer. "You've managed to make me feel better than I have in a long time. Thanks, Hank."

"I haven't done anything."

"But you have. You've given me your company, and I've been alone for a long time. Forever, it sometimes feels like."

"I know that feeling."

"I'm sure you do. And then you've offered to keep an eye on me. Maybe I'll actually be able to sleep tonight."

"You haven't been sleeping well?"

"Not at all, not since the attack. It's like part of me is always on the alert."

He figured he could understand that, too. And he could only think of one thing to do about it.

"Come on," he said. He pushed himself up off the couch, ignoring the way his body screeched at him. It never liked moving after it had been still for a while.

He reached out a hand and she took it, rising to face him.

Without a word, he led her down the hall to the spare room. "Crawl into bed," he said. "Sleep. I'll be right here to keep watch."

She shook her head, looking into his eyes as lightning flared again. "That's not fair to you."

"You can shut down your ears if another pair is doing your listening. No reason to think he'd look for you here, anyway."

No reason at all. Or so he told himself.

But since Kelly had entered his life, he'd been shaken out of the numb sense of disconnection he'd fostered. He cared again.

And while he said there was no reason for anyone to look for her at his house, he wished he was as sure of that as he sounded.

When she had finished changing into nightclothes and had climbed into the bed, she called to him.

He went to stand in the bedroom door and saw her pat the bed beside her. "Keep me company," she said. "I don't want to be alone. Just lie here with me?"

He wished he believed it would be as simple as that. He could have refused, but her unwillingness to be alone was something he was all too familiar with himself. The solitude of night could be the worst time.

Slowly, sure he was making a huge mistake, he walked over to the bed. This was going to be a trial by fire.

Chapter 8

Kelly lay beneath the covers, so he opted to kick off his work boots and lie on top of them beside her. His hip was still kicking up a ruckus, though, so he wound up lying on his side facing her.

At first that seemed safe enough. Buried under a quilt, lying on her back, she looked like Sleeping Beauty, unapproachable. The storm still grumbled outside, but the lightning was no longer as bright, nor the wind as strong. He tried to stare past her, at the curtained window, occupying himself by counting the time between flashes of light and rumbles of thunder. Tonight would not be a restful night for him, even in his own bed.

"Hank?"

"Yes?" He looked at her, but her eyes were still closed.

"Are you hurting?"

"A bit."

"So you won't be able to sleep?"

He wondered if she was seeking reassurance. "Not likely. There are nights like that sometimes."

"I'm sorry."

Then she floored him by rolling onto her side until their bodies nearly touched, and slipping an arm around him. "I wish I could make it go away."

She almost had. The things that were sizzling across his nerve endings now were more like the lightning from that storm than pain. He tightened his jaw against the unwanted surge of desire, thankful that quilts and clothing hid the obvious evidence of his reaction to her.

"It's getting better with time," he said, hoping she couldn't tell the words were coming from between clenched teeth.

"I'm glad to hear that. Not as bad or not as often?"

"Both."

"Would a massage help?"

A *massage?* The mere thought put his hormones into hyperdrive. God, yes, it would probably help, but the consequences were ones he didn't want to think about. He started counting reasons not to give in to passion: They'd only known each other a few days. She was probably seeking comfort more than anything because she felt so lonely. She was emerging from a bad marriage and probably had a whole knapsack load of stuff to deal with yet. One-night stands weren't his style and he doubted they were hers.

The one he avoided thinking about was the one that involved coming to care for her. Oh, he already cared for her, but not with the kind of depth that would blow him apart when she moved on.

Because she was going to move on as soon as she felt safe. She was going back to Miami for that divorce, and then she'd have a whole new life that he was sure wouldn't have anything to do with isolated Conard County and the husk of a cowboy.

Lots of reasons to climb off the bed right now and find a chair to sit in. Hell, he'd be safer on the floor, because right now she looked more like a looming threat of loss than a promise of paradise.

Then she shifted and started rubbing his back. Damn, that felt good. Too good.

"How's that?" she asked softly.

"Mmm." He didn't trust himself to say any more. He wanted to stay rigid, as if that were any defense, but the gentle circles she made on his back caused him to relax. Muscles that rarely seemed to let go anymore, let go, and his body began to feel like warm syrup.

Well, except for a certain member that started aching so hard, and throbbing so tightly, that it drove all thought of pain from his head.

In fact, it tried to drive *all* thought from his head. All those reasons he'd been counting in order to keep himself on the straight and narrow flitted further and further away with every movement of her hand.

He was losing it.

And then it was gone. All sense, all qualms, all his intelligence had vanished in a yearning that made everything else seem like a mere quibble.

He groaned, and felt her start to jerk back, as if she thought she'd hurt him. Every cell in his body protested the incipient separation, and without another thought he dove in and kissed her with every bit of the hunger he felt for her.

She gasped just as his mouth clamped over hers, and for an instant they shared one breath. But then she softened, her arm tightened around him, trying to pull him closer.

He was lost. And he was loving it. It had been so long, too long, since he'd wanted any woman, and he wanted this one more than most in his life.

He rolled a little, bringing them closer, urging her onto her back, managing to lift his leg over hers. Blankets and clothing still provided a barrier, but not enough of one to interfere with the moment—or the heat.

Her arms closed around his shoulders, welcoming him, as he plundered her mouth. She even tasted good, and the warmth of her tongue stroking his felt like heaven. He wanted to be deep within her, claiming her, taking her, riding her to the stars.

But some little bit of sense remained. Instead of giving in to the pulsing demand of his body, he chose instead to explore her hills and hollows with his hand. Her breast fit into his palm as if it had been made for him, and even through the cotton of her nightclothes he could feel her nipple pebbling, growing hard and big at the brush of his thumb.

Another spear of desired zapped him, causing him to drag his mouth from hers and close it over her breast, sucking both nipple and cotton into his mouth. He sucked gently at first, but when he heard her soft cry and felt her arch up toward him, he sucked even harder, filling his mouth with her, using his tongue to taunt her.

"Hank…" A breathy cry, sending a burst of triumph through him. She was his. He knew it. He sucked again, rhythmically, in time with the throb in his loins, and pressed his staff hard against her, slightly frustrated by the quilt that softened the contact. His hand traced her side, beginning to push away the quilt, seeking more delights along her waist, her hip.

And at that very instant his hip chose to erupt with searing agony.

He yanked away from her, swearing. Hell and damnation…

The last thing he wanted to do was roll away. The last thing he wanted to do was leave her there. But his hip showed no mercy.

The pain grabbed him until he was breathless with it, and he rolled away, needing to straighten out his leg, needing to move somehow to stop that godawful screech from angry nerves.

He pushed out of the bed. As he stood, his leg nearly gave way, but he mastered it, limping out of the room, limping anywhere, seeking any relief, trying to find the right movement, the right position, the right *anything*.

He hated himself. He hated thinking how he must have just made Kelly feel. Of all the stupid, cussed, idiotic things he could have done at such a moment…

"Hank? Is it your hip?"

He swung around and saw Kelly in the hallway. In another flare of lightning, he could see the wet spot he had made on her pajama top with his mouth.

"I'm sorry," he said, then continued his stomping walk as he tried to maneuver into a less painful position.

"No, *I'm* sorry," she said. "Are you sure massage won't help? Maybe some acupressure?"

"Acupressure?" Oh, man, that proved she came from a different world.

"Seriously," she said. "Sometimes if you press hard enough for a few seconds on a painful nerve, it'll quiet down. Let me at least try."

"I can't stop moving. It might freeze."

"Then I'll follow you around. Where is the worst pain?"

Reluctantly, he pointed to a spot on his hip between the pelvic bone and his buttocks. She hurried toward him.

"I'm going to poke. Tell me when I hit the most painful spot."

He forced himself to hold still, afraid that at any second it would tighten up so much that his leg would give way.

She poked hard at the area he had indicated. He winced.

She poked again nearby. "Let me know when it makes you want to scream."

He already wanted to scream, but then she hit the spot. He knew it. The pain drew a sharp groan from him. "There."

For an instant the world almost turned black as she dug her thumbs into the spot. If the pain had been bad before... He gritted his teeth, making himself endure, listening to her count the seconds. How long was he supposed to stand here? Dammit!

"Seven," she said, and pulled her thumbs away.

He almost jerked in surprise. The pain wasn't entirely gone, but it had diminished from excruciating to tolerable. "That helped."

"Don't sound so surprised. I actually learned that from a medical doctor."

He turned to face her, moving gingerly, afraid the pain would erupt again. "How does it work?"

"I don't remember the details. I just know it does. Usually when there's a spasm involved. I couldn't be sure it would help you, but I had to try."

"I'm glad you did." Extremely glad. "Wow!" He wiped the sweat from his forehead with his sleeve.

"That was bad, wasn't it?"

He felt after all that had just happened, he owed her honesty. "On a scale from one to ten, that was a twenty."

"I'm so, so sorry."

"No, I'm sorry for our interrupted interlude."

She looked down, but it was so dark he couldn't read her expression. If they were going to continue this conversation, he was going to need to turn on a light.

"I'm wide awake now," she said, lifting her head. "How about some coffee?"

"That won't help you sleep later."

"It's never stopped me before."

"Then coffee it is."

"I'll be right there." She turned and headed back to the bedroom, probably to change her damp pajama top. He couldn't blame her. Sometimes it was better to pretend things hadn't happened. And she had just as many reasons as he did for wanting to pretend right now.

He flipped on the kitchen light and started a pot of coffee brewing. While it brewed, he cussed himself again, because if he'd ever needed anything to remind him that he was the last person on whom Kelly should rely, it was what had just happened.

He'd keep her safe? Sure, as long as a bolt of pain didn't strike at the wrong moment. As long as his leg didn't give way just when it was needed. Damn, he hated himself, hated his unreliable body. How could he have been nuts enough to think there was any *possibility* that he could protect her? Why couldn't he stop deluding himself? He wasn't the man he used to be. There were things he simply could no longer do.

The coffee was half done when she reappeared wearing a yellow tank top and white shorts. Eye candy for sure, he thought, then forced his thoughts away from that. He'd just blown it big-time. No woman in her right mind could be interested in sex with a man who might leap out of bed like that without warning, leaving her unsatisfied.

Nope. Out of the question.

But she smiled as she sat at the table, waiting for her coffee. And he realized something else. She hadn't once suggested that he sit down, or that she should make the coffee. She hadn't treated him like an invalid. Not in the least little way.

Damn if he didn't appreciate that. It was a small bandage to his ego, but, right now, even the smallest one mattered.

She said not a word as he hobbled around getting the mugs,

carrying them to the table and filling them. Not a word except, "Thank you."

Taking the risk, he sat beside her. The ache was still there, the ache that might never go away, but he was no longer considering options like a chain saw to amputate himself.

"Thank *you*," he said.

"You might want to consider acupuncture," she offered. "Seriously. It works great for pain."

"I don't think we have anyone locally."

"That could be a problem. Most people need to go once a week or so. Of course, maybe someone here could learn to do it."

"Are you into a lot of New-Agey stuff?"

"There's nothing New Age about acupuncture, Hank. It works. It's an ancient form of medical treatment, and it works. Worth a try if you can get it."

He supposed it was. "I'll research it."

"Good." She reached out and covered his hand with hers. He liked the easy way she was willing to touch him, even after what had happened. At least he hadn't totally turned her off.

Although maybe it would have been better if he had.

"Anyway," she continued, "you'd have nothing to lose if you could find an acupuncturist who isn't too far away. If it helps, so much the better. But it's awful to see you hurt like that, and if it's awful to see, it must be so much worse for you."

"As I said, most of the time I can handle it. Every so often it just goes through the roof."

"Maybe all the work we've been doing on the house has aggravated things. Especially tearing up those floors." She shook her head. "I'm sorry. It's my fault. You weren't planning to do so much so fast."

"Blame Ben. He knew what he was renting to you."

"I can't blame Ben."

"Why not?"

"What else is he going to say when a woman he doesn't even know walks in and wants a rental for one or two months—no lease? How many places like that do you suppose are available around here?"

He sighed. "Probably not many."

"Probably none. He saw a chance to make a little money, and for you to make a little money, and he showed me the place first. It's not as if I didn't see it was a shambles."

"But there was stuff you didn't know about."

"And it's fixed. So maybe you should let up for a couple of days. I'll help carry all that flooring out to the trash when the bin arrives, and then we should take a break."

"I still need to do those windows on the porch, though. They're sitting in my garage just waiting for me to bump into them wrong."

"That was the next thing you planned to do, right?"

"Originally. It's not an awful job. With help it'll be almost easy."

"Well, I'll help. And then you should give yourself a day off. I'll even make you dinner, if you're willing to risk it."

"I'd like that." And he would. But he was rather amazed that he sensed absolutely no pulling away from her, despite the way he had left her in bed, aroused and unfulfilled. Most people would be hopping mad about that, or at least dismayed. Nothing about Kelly even suggested it.

Even so, it was another item to add to his list of reasons for avoiding anything even remotely romantic with Kelly. Her baggage, his baggage. And his was immutable.

Morning dawned bright, the sky so clear after the rain that everything appeared painfully sharp to the eye. Kelly looked out at the well-washed world, admiring it, and wondered if her own life would feel like that once everything to do with Dean lay in the past. Probably.

At least she hoped so. With morning came the nerve-crawling fear again, a feeling she couldn't shake for long, and less so now that she knew the real estate agent had run a credit check on her. Hank was right: They might as well have given out her address.

But she was safe here, in Hank's house, surely? At least for a while.

She had slept so well last night, the first good night's sleep she'd enjoyed since the attack. Hank hadn't lain down with her again. Even so, she'd been aware from time to time that he wasn't nearby, but before she really awoke to wonder, she heard his limping tread elsewhere in the house and knew he was there.

She smiled at him now as she walked into the kitchen and found him preparing a breakfast of bacon and eggs. "Thank you."

"For what?"

"I slept like a log."

He flashed a grin her way. "We aim to please."

"I haven't felt this good in forever. But what about you? Did you sleep at all?"

"I've become the world's greatest catnapper. I'm fine. There are some advantages to being a firefighter. One of them is you learn to sleep in snatches anywhere, any time, because you seldom get an uninterrupted night."

"That's a useful skill."

"It can be." He placed their already-filled plates on the table, poured some orange juice, and they sat to eat.

"I made some decisions," he announced as he reached for a slice of rye toast.

Kelly felt her stomach tighten. What kind of decisions did he have to make? Was he going to send her on her way?

Because after the last couple of days, she was more convinced than ever that she couldn't stand going on the road again. "What?" she finally asked.

"We're going to talk to the sheriff about your situation."

She put her fork down as the tightening in her stomach became painful. "He won't believe me."

Hank looked up from his plate. "This isn't Miami. This is a small town. Around here the sheriff isn't too busy to pay attention, and he's not likely to dismiss anything. Nor is he going to want to take a chance with your life."

"I don't know."

"Trust me on this, Kelly."

She *did* trust him, amazingly enough. It was the sheriff she wondered about. But she merely nodded.

"And then," he said, "we're going to have some fun. A little fun, anyway."

"What's that?"

"One of our local lights is a fantasy novelist. Amanda Tierney. Have you heard of her?"

"I don't read fantasy."

"Maybe you should start. I'm a big fan. Anyway, that's her pen name. Her real name is Amanda Laird, and she and her husband have a sheep ranch. I think you'll enjoy meeting her and some other folks from around here. And then maybe we can go to Maude's diner for a meal."

"You don't have to entertain me."

He lifted both eyebrows. "We've been working like dogs on the house, and I'm the only one who actually has to. Some welcome to the neighborhood. Hi, I'm your landlord, help me tear up floors and replace rotted joists."

The way he said it made her laugh and eased her apprehension a little. "But I don't know if I want so many people to know I'm here."

His face grew grave. "Kelly, at this point it doesn't make much difference, does it?"

Her heart sank a little, but she knew he was right. The anxiety didn't let up, wouldn't let up, and she was reasonably certain that Dean must have seen that her credit had been checked. Over four days ago. God, she didn't want to think about how much danger she might be in this very minute. But she told herself it was ridiculous to think she'd be any less safe on a public street in the middle of the day than she would be alone in her house.

"No," she said finally, "but I offered to make you dinner, remember? And you need a day off."

"I'm taking that day off *after* we talk to the sheriff. And after I get the new windows in. Then we can argue about book signings and dinner at Maude's."

She could see from the set of his jaw that he wasn't about to be budged, at least with regard to the sheriff. What's the worst that could happen? she asked herself. That she wouldn't be believed? That had already happened. If she could survive it the first time, she could survive it again, if for no other reason than to put Hank's mind at ease.

But all of a sudden, everything started closing in on her again. She had successfully managed to keep herself distracted enough that last night she'd blocked all thoughts of the guy who had tried to kill her. Well, almost completely blocked them. She'd managed to put them far enough in the background that she'd been able to feel almost normal.

But now she couldn't evade it anymore. It was still there, still hanging out, ugly and awful and frightening.

"It's going to be okay," Hank said, as if he read her feelings in her face.

"You can't promise that."

"No, I guess I can't. No one can and me maybe least of all,

given my leg. But does it help any to know that we're going to try to keep that promise? That I'm going to try to keep it?"

She looked at a man who had gone into a burning, unsafe building to try to save a woman, and knew deep in her heart that if she could trust anyone on this planet to protect her with everything he had, it was Hank Jackson.

But it didn't do a damn thing to ease her fear.

When they drove to the sheriff's office, Conard City still gleamed brightly from its overnight drenching. Pavement was still wet in places, and leaves shone freshly. Yards still sparkled with drops of water where the sun had not had time to dry them out.

It was, Kelly noted for the first time, a charming little town. It *did* look reliable—her first impression—but she supposed that mostly came from the older homes, the sense that they had endured for a long time and would continue to endure.

But now she noticed how pretty the big old trees were, turning the street along which they drove into a green canyon. It reminded her of the small town she had come from in central Florida, but not exactly. Nor could she put her finger on the difference she sensed. It was just different. Maybe it was just the difference in light, being so far north. Shadows here were longer, and deeper.

By the time Hank pulled into a parking place across the square from the courthouse, at a storefront clearly labeled *Conard County Sheriff's Office*, she had butterflies in her stomach. She definitely didn't want to do this.

But she was almost disarmed the instant Hank guided her through the front door. This was nothing like the police station she had gone to in Miami, brightly lighted, modern, overwhelmed by equipment and people. Instead, the dispatcher sat right up front, evidently doubling as the duty officer. A woman of indeterminate age, with a weathered face, looked at her through a cloud of cigarette smoke and smiled.

"This is Velma," Hank said, making introductions. "If she ever leaves this desk, nobody knows."

"Ha!" Velma's laugh was short and sharp, and her voice cracked from years of smoking. "I'll be buried in this chair."

"Probably." Hank grinned. "Is Gage around?"

"He's around almost as much as I am. You know where his office is."

Kelly followed Hank down a narrow hallway, where he stopped and rapped on a door to the left.

A voice from within called, "Come on in."

Hank pushed the door open and Kelly got her first glimpse of the sheriff of Conard County. He said behind a desk, clad in the local tan uniform, just like his deputies, but his face almost caused her to gasp. One side of it bore the shiny scar tissue of a serious burn than ran down his neck to disappear into his collar. His welcoming smile was just a little crooked, probably because of the burn.

"Good to see you, Hank. What's up?"

"This is Kelly Scanlon. She has reason to believe her husband may be trying to have her killed."

The sheriff's smile vanished. "Have a seat."

The nameplate on the front of his desk said, *Gage Dalton, Sheriff.* Kelly focused on it like a lifeline. She was afraid she would see disbelief in the sheriff's face.

"Want to tell me about it?"

Kelly hesitated. No, she didn't want to tell him about it. Every time she said it out loud it sounded crazier than the last time.

Hank finally spoke. "Kelly rented the house next to mine, which is how I met her."

"That old run-down place?"

"We're fixing it. You have a problem, talk to Ben. He rented it while I was out on the range at the Russell ranch."

"Ben. It figures." Gage snorted. "Go on."

Hank waited a moment, as if giving her a chance to speak, but she still wasn't quite ready. Another cop, another person who wouldn't believe her. The amazing thing was that Hank believed her.

So he did the talking, at first anyway. He sketched the situation for Gage, including the email from his friend on the Denver police, and the fact that Ben had done a credit check on her. Then he added what she considered the real kicker upon reflection: the fact that her attacker had carried her to the canal where she often ran before trying to drown her.

Then she heard something she had never expected to hear from a cop. "This doesn't sound good," Gage said. "I wish you'd come to me right away, Ms. Scanlon."

At that she lifted her head and looked at him for the first time since entering the room. "Why would I go to the police? They didn't believe me in Miami."

"This isn't Miami." Gage gave her that crooked smile. "I worked for DEA there, you know."

"Really?"

"Really. And I can tell you why the cops put you off. They hear countless stories like this every day, and most of the time it truly is just a random mugging with little hope of finding the perp. It doesn't mean they didn't care that you were attacked. It's just that with no evidence to build a case, there's not much else they can do."

"I know." She sighed. "Believe me, I've had plenty of time to think about it."

"That visit to your husband to question him though..." Gage trailed off thoughtfully. "I'm not sure that was the best tactical decision. In their shoes I would have wanted to place him under surveillance for a while, rather than warn him. But my background is different, and their resources are pretty limited. Their plate is overflowing, you could say."

"I guess."

"Big city police departments are often overworked. They usually do a good job despite that, but they have to prioritize things. How soon after the attack did you leave town?"

"Two days. I felt like a sword was hanging over my head."

He nodded. "I can understand that. Unfortunately, that limited their options. They couldn't put surveillance on you because you were gone. They could question your husband, as a kind of warning, but that was it."

"Oh." She hadn't thought of that. "Nobody said anything about watching me."

"They wouldn't have. And now that you're out of Miami, you're not their concern anymore. Now you're mine."

A flicker of hope sprang to life in her heart. "You believe me?"

"Of course I believe you. I don't think anyone ever disbelieved you, Ms. Scanlon. The problem was proving something. They couldn't prove that your husband was behind the attack, they couldn't find the attacker…and then you hightailed it. Case closed, for now anyway. At this point, right now, *I* can't be sure your husband was behind the attack on you. Neither can you. But I'm not willing to dismiss the possibility. He threatened you, and then you were attacked in a very odd way. No, I'm not going to dismiss it. Not at all."

Kelly unleashed a shaky sigh, and felt her tension ease once again. "Thank you. I've been so scared."

"I imagine so."

"I've spent a lot of time wondering if I was all wrong about it, too."

"Well, I guess we'll probably find out, because it's been what, four or five days since Ben did that credit check? If someone is after you, he should be here soon. And the nice thing about this town is that strangers get noticed pretty quickly. I'm going to have you talk to our sketch artist…"

"We could just get the sketch from Miami," Hank said.

Gage shook his head. "I don't want to risk sending up another flare that Ms. Scanlon is here or announce that she's contacted us. I want some time to get ready, and there's already very little if someone is determined to get her soon. The only thing I can see that we have going for us is that the court hearing isn't for two months. That takes the time pressure off her husband."

"What are you going to do?"

"The surveillance that Miami PD should have done. Might have done. Everyone in the department is going to be alerted. We'll keep an eye on Ms. Scanlon, and an eye out for her attacker."

Kelly hesitated, then asked, "Wouldn't it be better if it got around that I'd spoken to you?"

Gage looked almost grim as he shook his head. "That depends. It would make you safer while you're here. But when you leave? What then?"

"So…it's better to draw him here?" The idea made her feel those hands around her throat all over again. She had to close her eyes for a moment as a shudder of horror ran through her.

"If you want this finished, yes. At least here you'll have a lot of people looking after you."

Chapter 9

"How do you feel now?" Hank asked when they were back in his truck. "Any better?"

"Yes. Yes, I guess I do feel better. Except for the part where I'm going to feel like bait. But the sheriff was right. If I just move on without settling this, there's still two more months to worry about. At least. And if I went back to Miami for the court appearance, I'd be scared out of my wits."

"I want you to go back for that appearance."

"Why?" She turned in her seat to look at him.

"Because after what that bastard put you through, I think you deserve every penny you can get out of him."

A little laugh escaped her. "I thought that at first, too. Now I just want to be rid of him."

"That's what he's probably hoping."

"How do you mean?"

"Well, suppose he just paid that guy to scare you, not kill you. What's the likelihood you'd show up in court?"

Her jaw dropped a little. "You have a devious mind."

"I'm just trying to think things through. Maybe he wants you dead. Maybe he wants you not to show up. Maybe he thinks that if you don't show up it would mean you've given up on a big settlement and he can get it down to something like your attorney's fees."

"Man!" Her exclamation was appalled. "The worst part of it is, I can imagine Dean thinking just like that. Well, I'm going back for that appearance."

"You made up your mind?"

"You bet."

"Then we'd better keep our eye out for a killer."

He turned over the ignition and started to back out of the parking space. "If you don't want to go to that book signing, I'll just run in and get Mandy to sign the book for me."

That made her feel about two inches tall. This man had upended his life for her, had offered to protect her—and that was no lightweight offer from a man like him—he'd invited her into his home, into his life and now she was going to cut short something he'd obviously been looking forward to?

"No, I'd like to go." She *did* feel better after talking to the sheriff, and she felt safe with Hank. Nobody would try to abduct her while she was with him. Plus, there'd be other people around. It would be nice to meet a few of them, especially since, at the back of her mind, she was having thoughts of staying here once the divorce was final.

Silly thoughts, she told herself. Born, most likely, of how safe Hank made her feel. And that was a lousy reason to decide to settle somewhere. Once the divorce was over, she'd have nothing to fear any longer. She could choose to live anywhere she wanted, including in Miami, right under Dean's nose, if she could stand being that close to him.

The thought almost made her laugh.

Bea's Bookstore was tiny and smelled richly of books.

They seemed to fill almost every inch of space, leaving just enough room to maneuver through aisles. At the back, though, were a couple of easy chairs and a wooden reading table where an attractive woman in her forties sat with a stack of hardcover books in front of her.

"Mandy," Hank said with real pleasure. "Do I get the first copy?"

The woman laughed. "Saved just for you." Her gaze trailed to Kelly. "I don't think we've met."

"Kelly Scanlon," Hank said. "My new tenant. She just moved here."

Mandy reached out to shake her hand. "Welcome to town. I hope you love it here as much as most of us do."

"I'm falling in love with it already."

"No Ransom this morning?" Hank asked as he lifted a copy of the book.

"Someone had to stay home with the kids. And I don't mean the goats." Mandy's eyes were sparkling. "We raise sheep and goats," she explained to Kelly. "And all three of the human kids woke up under the weather this morning. Apparently, they caught a case of the 'something that's going around.'"

Kelly laughed. "There's a lot of that everywhere."

Hank picked up a second copy of the book. "I'm going to get one for Kelly, too. I know she'll enjoy your work as much as I do."

Ten minutes later, having met the store's owner and a handful of others who had come for the signing, Kelly emerged again into the sunlight with Hank, and paused on the sidewalk to look up and down the street.

"I like how friendly people are here," she announced.

"Most folks are," he agreed. "See that sign for the City Diner? Everyone here refers to it by the owner's name.

Maude's we call it. Want to stop in for coffee and a light lunch?"

"Sure. And thank you for the book."

"You're welcome."

His smile, she thought, was charming. Always charming. It wasn't the pretended social affability she had seen too much of. When Hank Jackson smiled, it seemed to emanate from his very soul.

Hugging her book, feeling as if she'd just been given a wonderful gift, perhaps the most wonderful she had ever received, she walked slowly with him down the street.

"You *do* seem to feel better," he remarked as he limped at her side.

"I do. Talking to the sheriff was a good idea. He not only seems to know what he's doing, but I get the feeling he cares."

"That he does. There was a time when he was a stranger here, too. Never talked to anybody. Folks used to call him Hell's Own Archangel."

"Really?" That astonished her. "Not very kind."

"I think it had to do with the anger and grimness people felt in him. He'd lost his wife and kids to a car bomb set by one of the drug dealers he was after. And, obviously, he was injured, too."

"You two must have a lot to talk about."

"Sometimes," he agreed. "Sometimes."

She heard the door close on the subject, so she dropped it.

Maude's diner proved to be an interesting place. Leaning toward Hank in the booth after Maude took their orders and gave them coffee, Kelly murmured, "I don't think I've ever had my coffee slammed down like that before."

"Maude's a piece of work," he agreed with a twinkling

eye. "It's a good thing you knew what you wanted to eat or she'd have made up your mind for you."

Kelly sat back, absorbing this very different environment. Of course, Dean never would have taken her to a place like this, so déclassé, but she could see with a quick scan that there was someone at almost every table, and many older men and women clustered in groups over coffee and deep in discussion. Apparently, Maude's was the place to go.

Her choice of a piece of cobbler was slammed down in front of her with as much emphasis as the coffee and she found herself looking into Maude's gimlet eye.

"This one," Maude announced to Hank, "needs looking after. Hear?"

"I hear," he answered.

"Good." Then Maude sailed on, back toward the kitchen from which the clanging of pots and the rattle of dishes could be heard.

Kelly leaned toward Hank again. "Who runs this town?"

He chuckled. "Depends. The mayor thinks he does, the sheriff mostly does, along with Velma, but Maude runs anything they don't…like what you're going to eat when you walk through that front door."

She laughed and felt the day grow even brighter. She liked it here, she liked everyone she'd met, even Maude, and she just wished the cloud hanging over her head would go away. Permanently.

Hank noted that Kelly's mood seemed to sink as they went home. Well, of course. It brought back the entire reason she was here, and the only reason she was staying. She'd been able to forget for a little while, but now here it was in her face again.

"You're taking the day off to rest, right?" she asked as they pulled into his driveway.

He thought about the windows for the mudroom, then took an internal inventory. He sighed. "Yup. No work today."

She turned in the seat so that she faced him. "Does it frustrate you?"

"Sometimes. It wasn't very long ago that when I said *go*, my body got up and went. It takes a little more planning now. And sometimes I just need to be smart and not do anything at all."

"That *would* be frustrating," she agreed.

"But before we settle in to read our books or whatever, I want to check the caulking."

"I thought you said the rain wouldn't hurt it."

"It shouldn't have, but I still want to check. Wait here. It'll only take a minute."

She followed his directions, understanding already that he was a man who didn't want to be made to feel like an invalid, but it was getting so that when she saw him limp, she hurt for him. Some things, she thought, could change your life forever in just a few seconds or minutes. Like her abduction and near drowning. Like having a building collapse on you and losing two friends. Nothing would ever be the same again, no matter how you tried to put your life back together.

Like now. She couldn't stop looking nervously around, wondering if her killer could be hiding somewhere right this minute, waiting for his chance.

Hank returned in five minutes. "Caulking is fine," he smiled, and together they went into his house. As they stepped on the porch, another rumble of thunder reached them and he paused to look southward.

"Weird," he said.

"What is?"

"We don't get a lot of rain here. We're in the rain shadow of the mountains, so we stay pretty dry. Two storms in two days?"

"Climate change," she suggested.

"Climate chaos, more like." He twisted the key in the door and waved her in ahead of him. "We've been getting more snow in the winters so, yeah. Why should I be surprised if we get more rain in the summers?"

Inside, he closed and locked the door, then faced her with a smile. "Okay, I'm taking that rest day you insisted on. So how do you want to spend it? We can read, play cards, watch movies or sit out back and get sunburned."

The notion of sitting outside didn't appeal to her, in part because she would feel exposed, and partly because the temperatures here were so much cooler than she was used to in Miami that she couldn't imagine sunning herself.

"I'd be out there bundled up in your sweatshirt."

"That's what I forgot. I was going to take you by Freitag's Mercantile so you could get a sweater or something. Not that they're probably selling much in the way of cool-weather clothing right now."

"I'll give you your sweatshirt back," she offered hastily. "It must bother you to see me wearing it."

"That's not what I meant. It doesn't bother me at all or I wouldn't have gotten it out. No, I just thought you'd like to have something that fits better."

The truth was, she loved being swallowed by his sweatshirt. Overnight it had come to feel like a security blanket. "It's fine. I love it. So let's not go racing to the store right now."

He gave her a mock frown. "You're interfering with my every attempt not to be indolent."

"I hardly think an afternoon off is indolence."

The frown eased into a smile. "Coffee and cards? Or coffee and books? Or movies. Or whatever."

Her mind chose a path on that *whatever* that almost made her blush. She'd been trying since he rolled out of bed in agony last night not to think about what had started between them, and she didn't dare mention it, even if lying in his arms in that bed sounded like the best thing in the world to her. Of all the options, she would have chosen *whatever*. But she couldn't even guess if he felt the same way.

"Definitely coffee," she said after a moment. "And maybe some cards? I haven't played in a long time, and I'm not ready yet to settle in to a book."

They played Hearts, but the conversation didn't revolve around cards.

"That's awful—what happened to your sheriff," she remarked.

"I know. Every time I've even wandered close to self-pity, I've thought about Gage. Wife and kids, and he was standing right there when it happened. Cripes."

"But things are better for him now?"

"Much. He married our librarian, known to everyone as Miss Emma, and they've adopted a couple of children. He told me once that he was so scared of losing kids that for a long time he wouldn't even consider it. And for a long time after they got their first, he hovered over the baby constantly, frightened that something might happen."

She nodded. "And you? Do you feel the same way?"

He stared at his cards and finally looked at her. "For a while I did. I had resolved to become a hermit."

"And after that an old curmudgeon?"

He flashed a grin. "That was the next option. Unfortunately, being a hermit doesn't exactly suit me, and I still can't bring myself to yell at the kids for playing on my lawn."

"You've got a lot of work to do on that image."

"Tell me about it. It might help me develop if a baseball came flying through a window, but the kids tend to play in the park two blocks over, so I've given up on that ever happening."

"I could go ask one to do it."

He shook his head. "Don't bother. I'd just replace the window."

At that she laughed wholeheartedly. "You're funny, Hank Jackson."

He put a hand over his heart. "I think I'm wounded."

"Hardly. You're a softie. You'd no more yell at a kid than you would have told me to get lost once you knew I was in trouble. Heck, even before you knew you didn't throw me out of that house. And you could have. No, you just went to work to make it safe. And now look at you. Your hermitage has been invaded. By your own invitation."

"Just don't tell anyone. I'm working on it, okay?"

"Yeah, right."

He chuckled again. Then their eyes locked across the table, and the laughter faded. After a moment he said, "Um, so are you going to pick up your life in Miami after the divorce is settled?"

A few weeks ago, she might have said yes. Maybe even a few days ago. "I lived in Florida all my life. It's what I know. But…"

"But?"

"I'm not sure anymore. So far I like it here. And I probably shouldn't admit it, but I like not being hot all the time. I didn't expect that."

Another couple of moments ticked by, their gazes still locked. "Why didn't you expect it?" he asked.

"Because I'm so used to the weather down there. And I always hate it when it gets cold and nothing I do seems to keep me warm. Except…I like the coolness here."

"It can get awful in the winters if you're not used to it."

"I expect so. But I could probably get used to it."

"I'm sure you could." He leaned back a bit, breaking the eye contact that had begun to make her oddly breathless. "More coffee?"

"Please."

He emptied both their cups, getting rid of what had cooled down and replacing it with fresh, hot brew. "So you're thinking about a major life change," he remarked as he sat across from her again. "This place seems a bit out of the way and slow for someone from Miami."

"That's part of what I like about it. I guess my only problem would be finding a job. How many medical billing clerks can you need around here?"

"I don't know. You might ask at the hospital if the urge to stay keeps growing on you. We have kind of a brain drain. Young folks get out of here as fast as they can. Off to bigger cities or colleges, and they seldom come back."

"That's sad."

He shrugged one shoulder. "I did it myself. For a while the drain slowed down. The junior college still helps, and the semiconductor plant stemmed the tide to almost nothing, but then they started laying people off. So, you know, they might actually need a billing clerk at the hospital. Or I guess you could train for a different career at the college. If you decide to stay."

If she decided to stay. She made a show of picking up her cards again, but she didn't really see them. The urge to plant herself here permanently was growing, but she couldn't be certain why. Maybe it was Hank. Maybe it was feeling, for the first time in ages, that someone actually gave a damn about her.

It seemed like a nice town, but there were lots of nice towns. If this urge she was feeling hinged on Hank…well, that could wind up being a stupid thing to do. Other than wanting to make love to her—and she wasn't even completely certain about that—he'd given her no reason to think he wanted her to hang around.

He was just being a nice guy.

And why that should sadden her so much, she couldn't begin to say.

Hank noticed her mood change, and ran their conversation back in his mind, trying to figure out if he'd said something. But no, it had been merely a casual conversation about staying here in Conard County. No big deal that he could see…unless that was it. Maybe the thought of restarting her life had saddened her all over again. That wouldn't be surprising.

But then she surprised him with the turn of her thoughts. "You know what you said about how maybe Dean just wanted to scare me?"

"Yeah?"

"I don't think so. He'd already agreed to the settlement. Which, according to my lawyer, was as good as having it cast in stone at that point. And my lawyer said something else. He said that if I tried to lower the amount, no judge would agree because he or she would be certain I'd been intimidated."

"Ah. I didn't think of that, but it makes sense."

"Well, wouldn't Dean's lawyer have made that clear to him, too, that once he signed a settlement agreement it was as good as done?"

"You're right." He hated to say it, only now realizing how much he had been cherishing a hope that this whole thing would blow over without any more trouble for her. "I'm not a lawyer."

One corner of her mouth tugged briefly upward, in a smile that couldn't quite make it. "Sorry, I guess I can't forget about it for very long. Now I've ruined the mood."

What mood, he wondered. Something had cast her down, the minute they started talking about her future plans. It wasn't as if they'd been having some kind of riotous party and she'd burst into tears inexplicably. "You didn't ruin anything. We were just playing cards. I imagine that thinking about all the changes ahead of you isn't easy."

"It's easier than thinking that creep might be on my tail." She sighed and pushed her cards aside. "I just want it over. I'm tired of the whole mess. I am *so* ready to move on."

Move on to where? But there was no answer to that yet. He doubted that she would want to stay here once she got to know the place. Oh, there was no better place than this for raising a family, making friends, settling down. But she was used to a different kind of life. Conard County would probably bore her to tears once she saw enough of it.

But amid his concern for her, he felt a niggle of concern for himself. He was getting involved here, however casually, with someone who would leave. He needed his head examined. Hadn't losing Fran been lesson enough?

Unfortunately, that argument didn't seem to be working as well anymore. Now that he was mostly past survivor guilt, it was beginning to sound a bit puerile—even to him. Bad things happened to everyone. Picking up your toys and going home never to play again was a childish response. Useless, too. Life had landed on his doorstep and, if nothing else, it was time to realize that he *was* still alive.

And if, given the same set of circumstances, he would still go into that building to save a woman's life, then maybe he needed to get around to honestly forgiving himself. Not just saying it, but believing it. He hadn't asked Fran or Allan to follow him. They had made that decision the same way he had made his own.

He suddenly froze as a dawning understanding hit him.

"Hank? What's wrong?"

Part of him wanted to keep the new understanding private.

Yet a bigger part of him needed to share it, to test it against the response of another human being.

"I just…realized something," he said.

"Yes?" Her blue eyes were concerned, gentle. Such gentle eyes. He was glad that tenderness had survived her marriage.

"I just realized that I didn't ask Fran and Allan to come into that building with me. I never even glanced their way. They made their own decision to go with me."

"Yes." She nodded, then waited, as if she knew there was more.

"Well, I never thought of it quite this way before, but it just struck me: By taking the blame for what happened to them, by feeling that it's all my fault they're gone, I dishonor them."

"Dishonor them how?"

"By not recognizing they were capable of making their own decision to help save that woman. That they were doing what firefighters do, just as I was. And to think they went in only because of me does them no honor at all. They would have gone whether I had or not."

She nodded slowly. "You're right. Looking at it that way *does* honor them. And I agree. They weren't kids just tagging along, were they? No, they were experienced firefighters, too."

"Yes. They were. Great ones." He drew a long breath and let go of some deep pain that never left him. "I guess that's what they call an epiphany."

"It sounds like it." She reached for her cards and began swirling them on the table, pointlessly, except possibly to occupy her hands. "You told me to stop second-guessing myself. You even said that if you were in exactly the same circumstances, knowing what you knew then and not what you know now, that you would have gone into that building."

"I did."

Her smile was faint. "Your friends evidently reached the same conclusion. "Can you even be sure you were the first one to move?"

"No. Heat, smoke, face mask…I didn't see them until we were inside. And then it was too late."

"So maybe you all moved at once. I admit, I don't get being a firefighter. But going into situations like that seems to be what firefighters do."

He gave a short nod. What was there to say? Anyone who couldn't do *exactly* that didn't make it much past training.

"My guess would be that you all made exactly the same decision at exactly the same moment when you heard there was a woman inside."

"Maybe."

She pursed her lips, but he could still see a smile there. "No maybe about it. They were good firefighters. You said so yourself."

And that was the crux of the matter right there. All three of them had had the same instinct and responded in the same way. They hadn't exchanged a word or a look. They'd just gone in.

"What if you hadn't gone in, but they had?" she asked. "Somehow I don't think you'd feel any better about this."

No, for a fact. He was sure of that. He closed his eyes a moment, his head suddenly filled with the captain's crackling voice as it had come over the radio just seconds before the collapse. "Get out. Get out now. The structure is about to go."

But there hadn't been time. They'd turned around, facing the inevitable: that they wouldn't be able to save the trapped woman if the building was falling. And that was all he remembered.

"Okay," he said. "Enough of that. I don't want to go back there."

"I'm sure you don't."

"So let's talk about you."

"Me? What about me?"

"Well, it seems like a good time for building castles in the air. You're about to shuck Dean and start fresh. There has to be *something* good in that."

"I may feel more like it once it's past." But she seemed to shake herself a little, as if redirecting her thoughts. "I haven't really done a lot of thinking about it."

"Why not?"

"Well, first, the divorce was looming. I got myself this little apartment, managed to get hired as a waitress because no other doctor wanted to touch me while I was divorcing Dean, and I just wasn't thinking about much except getting through it. I guess I assumed I'd just keep living in that apartment, find a permanent job and go on pretty much the way I was."

"Except for old friends."

A short, mirthless laugh escaped her. "Yeah, they sure vanished into the woodwork fast enough. I broke the unwritten code, I guess."

"Which is?"

"Never divorce a wealthy older man." But then she frowned. "And maybe that's not entirely fair. I mean, I'm sure it made them uncomfortable in a lot of ways. Being around someone going through that kind of emotional upheaval isn't fun."

"But that's when true friends stick."

"You'd think." She shook her head again. "Some of them got really angry at me. But the one who made me angriest of all was Jill. She said she wouldn't judge me."

"Hah! That sounds like she already had."

"That's what I thought. Didn't ask for my side or anything. Just said she wouldn't judge me. Gee, thanks."

"So not even one stuck around?"

"No. But then, they were all people I got to know because

of Dean. It's not like any of them were *my* friends. And working in his office, I didn't get a chance to meet anyone he didn't know."

"Yeah, that would complicate it. So you must have felt truly alone."

"I did."

He knew that feeling. It didn't necessarily come from friends deserting you. It could even happen among friends who were trying to be supportive, simply because they couldn't understand. In the end, he had been the one who'd abandoned his friends. He shifted uncomfortably.

And all of a sudden he needed to get up, move around, *do* something. He rose from the table. "I'm going to walk around outside."

"Do you want company?"

He hesitated. There was still this amorphous threat hanging over her, the uncertainty about whether a killer might show up at any moment. Better to be together, he decided. If that guy showed up, bent on finishing the job, he'd most likely try when she was alone.

"Sure," he said. He was getting uncomfortable inside his own skin, but her presence wasn't going to change that one way or another. He needed movement, action, the way plants needed the sun. Life might force him to be sedentary sometimes, but he didn't have to like it.

Building storm clouds and increasing wind added a wild element to the day that he savored. Rare enough that he got to enjoy weather like this around here. Together they walked past her rental house. He figured he'd take a turn around the block and see how he felt about going farther.

He always wanted to go farther these days. And it was always a trade-off about how much he wanted to pay for it later. His doc kept saying it would improve in time, but nobody was willing to say how much it would improve, or even when. Maybe it was just a matter of getting used to it.

The tang of ozone in the air tickled his nose. He glanced over at Kelly and saw that she had her eyes half-closed and her head tipped back a bit, as if she were soaking it all in. So she liked it, too.

For some reason, that made him reach for her hand, and his heart eased a little as he felt her welcome his touch by twining her fingers with his.

All the demons of caution shut up for a little while and he was glad. Had to be something seriously wrong with you if you couldn't just enjoy holding a woman's hand as you strolled down the street.

Nobody was out and about, except for an occasional car passing slowly on the street. While lots of folks around here enjoyed walking on nice days, with a storm rolling in, they'd choose their cars for that quick run to the store or library.

He decided to go farther, until they reached the park. It was unusually deserted for a Saturday, and given that the march of thunder was getting louder, he opted not to linger, although another time it might be fun to push Kelly on the swing.

If Kelly was still around. Dammit, that thought darkened his mood more than it should have. What was going on here?

But before he could ponder that cosmic question, a patrol car came by and pulled up beside them. Deputy Beauregard leaned out. "How's it going, Hank?"

"Just great."

"This must be Ms. Scanlon?"

"Hi," Kelly said.

Beau gave her a salute, finger to the brim of the cowboy hat he wasn't wearing inside the car. Even without the hat, the gesture worked. "Pleased to make your acquaintance, ma'am. Just keeping an eye out."

"Thank you." Kelly's reply sounded heartfelt.

"Just doing my job, ma'am."

Talk turned to the unusual weather for a few moments, then Beau drove on.

"They really *are* watching," Kelly remarked.

"Yup. We've got us a good sheriff's department here." He squeezed her hand gently as they continued their walk.

That's when he realized what had truly made him antsy. It wasn't thinking about the past. It was that smoky desire he felt around her and tried so hard to ignore. It was an urge to fall into bed with her and finish what they had begun last night. That and that alone had made it impossible for him to sit still a moment longer. Damn, he wanted this woman.

And he had no idea if she felt the same way. Yes, she'd seemed to last night, but that was last night and he'd ruined it by tumbling out of bed because of his hip.

She'd probably be relieved if he never touched her again after that.

Which soured his mood beyond belief. Overreact much? he asked himself. But the question didn't help, and the mood didn't improve.

"Do you want me to stay with you tonight?" she asked.

Aw, hell. Yes and no. Yes because he was worried about her. Yes because he wanted her. No because he was afraid passion might overtake him again.

"I can stay at my place," she said quickly. "I just need to know whether I should get more clothes."

He gave up before he'd even waged the battle. "Let's get you more clothes."

"Thanks. I really appreciate it."

"Well, considering that Ben made a total hash of it by doing that credit check…" Good excuse but not the complete truth. Not even Fran had made him feel this mixed up. But of course, with Fran, things had been simpler. No shadowy killers, no half-finished divorce, no warning signs that she was going to hit the road any day.

He waited while she unlocked the front door and together they stepped into her house. And both of them halted in the same instant.

She turned to him swiftly. "Someone was in here."

He smelled it. "What the hell kind of killer wears cologne?"

It hung on the air, faint and threatening. And it was undeniable.

Kelly began to shake. She recognized the odor. She recognized it even more clearly than she would have recognized the face of the man who had attacked her. "It's him," she said, barely a whisper.

Hank swore. Without another word, he tried to pull her out of the house.

"No," Kelly said. "No." She pulled free and looked around. There was a hammer lying on the floor and she picked it up. "He's not scaring me off again," she said quietly.

So Hank grabbed a screwdriver from the window ledge. "We should call the cops," he muttered.

"Not yet. If that SOB is in my house, I want my licks first."

The statement appeared to startle Hank a bit, but she ignored it. Her mind was focused on one thing and one thing only: That man had knocked her on the head and tried to drown her. And if she got anywhere near him, she was going to make him regret it.

Step by quiet step, they worked their way through the house, front to back. At least there was no upstairs to worry about. Well, an attic, but that wasn't foremost in her mind.

If the guy was up there, he wasn't going to come down now because she wasn't alone.

And she was so grateful that Hank was with her. He was moving as quietly as possible, given his limp, but that irregular gait behind her reassured her. This time she was not alone in some parking garage or at canal-side. This time she had backup.

Still, this was the scariest thing she'd done in her life, creeping through a house looking for an intruder. Every doorway presented a threat, every closet held a dark secret. One by one they checked them all and found no one. The house appeared empty.

She looked at Hank. "The attic."

"I'm no chicken, but I'm not poking my head up through an attic door, and neither are you. If he's up there, he's trapped for now. So now it's time to get a cop out here."

She leaned back against the wall and let him make the call, her eyes fixed on the attic door in the bedroom ceiling. Funny, she'd never noticed it before. Certainly she hadn't worried about it.

But now it looked dangerous. Very dangerous. A killer could be behind it.

Five minutes later, Gage Dalton arrived in the company of another deputy. To Kelly's surprise, they were both dressed in jeans and light jackets, not uniforms.

"Figured it was best not to advertise," Gage said when he saw her look. "Just in case. So you smelled him?"

"I smelled his cologne," she agreed. "I'll never forget that smell. He wears too much of it."

"However much he wears," Gage answered, "we remember smells better than faces. This is Deputy Locke. So we need to check the attic?"

"Please."

The sheriff looked at Locke. "You're young."

Locke half smiled. "That's one way of phrasing it."

"All right, you have a harder head. Go grab a chair."

Laughing with quiet good humor, the deputy went in search of a chair. Gage looked up at the attic door. "Is that the only way in?"

"Yup," Hank answered. "Not likely anyone could get in there without leaving some sign behind. Like a chair."

"Yeah, but it never pays to overlook something like that." He returned his attention to Kelly, who had her arms wrapped around herself, feeling cold to the bone. She'd left the hammer on the bed.

"You don't have to stay," he said. "You can go home with Hank, if you'll feel better."

"I have to know."

Gage nodded, understanding.

Deputy Locke returned with a kitchen chair and climbed on it, pushing the board that sealed the attic up and in. Gage passed him a flashlight from his jacket pocket, and they waited while he scanned the space.

"Nothing's been up here recently," Locke said. "Dust rules. I like it better than rain for giving away a perp."

He lowered the door back into place and climbed down.

"Thanks, Locke," Gage said. "Look around outside, will you? But take a clipboard so you look like some kind of workman. There's one in my car."

"Sure thing."

Questions were mounting in Kelly's mind as the first shock passed. "Why are you pretending not to be cops?"

"In case he's watching. We don't want him to know we're in on this. The easier he thinks it'll be to get at you, the more likely he is to help us catch him."

She nodded. That made sense to her, especially since she had realized she had only two choices: One was to run again and try to stay alive for the next two months, and the other was to stick it out here and hope to catch the guy so she didn't have to keep looking over her shoulder. And having been on the run, it was not something she wanted to do again if she could avoid it.

"Look around inside," Gage suggested. "See if he tampered with anything."

Thankful for something to do, Kelly wandered through the house, trying to remember how she'd left everything. The task proved difficult, considering that the house was still half torn up and awaiting the arrival of the big trash bin to get rid of the flooring. But she hadn't brought much with her to begin with, and a search of the two dresser drawers she was using didn't indicate that anyone had gone into them. If they had, they hadn't moved anything.

"Nothing," she said finally in the kitchen.

Gage spoke. "He may have just been scoping the place. You were out, right?"

"Since yesterday," Hank volunteered. Kelly nearly blushed at the implication, but Gage didn't seem to take notice of it at all.

"He could have entered any time then. I know if I were him, I'd want to know the layout and where obstacles were." He leaned back against the counter and folded his arms. "So, the question is what do we do now?" He looked at Kelly, as if awaiting her judgment.

"You're asking me? I'm not a cop."

"No, I'm asking you what outcome you want to see. Do you want to stay, now that you know he's here? Do you want us to try to end it here? Or do you want to move on?" He paused. "Before you answer, keep in mind that my department isn't omniscient or omnipotent. You're in danger. I have no way to guarantee with complete certainty that you won't get hurt, no matter what we do."

She appreciated his honesty, even though she'd already

pretty much figured that out. "You know," she said, "I've had enough of Dean and his machinations. I've had enough of him ruining my life one way or another. All he had to do was let me go. He started this mess, but I'm going to finish it."

She didn't miss the way the two men smiled at her. She hoped they weren't looking at her like a mouse who was pretending to be a lion, roaring with nothing to back it up.

"Okay then," Gage said. "I'm going to get you a beeper. Wear it around your neck. If anything at all makes you uneasy, push the button. I'll have everyone on alert and keep at least two people nearby at all times. If that beeper goes off, we're coming. And I don't want you to ever hesitate to use it. Promise?"

"I promise."

Gage looked at Hank. "Is she going to be staying at your place again tonight?"

"Do you think it makes a difference?"

"Unfortunately, yes. She has to appear to be alone here, and unprotected."

"Then you'd better give me one of those beepers, too, so I can tell if she's in trouble. I can make it over here lickety split."

"Fair enough. I'll get you a receiver, too."

Locke returned, useless clipboard in hand. "He came in by way of the mudroom window. I can see the scraping where he worked on the lock."

"Well, damn," Hank said. "I knew I should have gotten to those sooner. I'll replace them today. The new windows can't be jimmied easily."

Kelly reached out and touched his arm. "No. Let him think he knows how to enter. Let him do it. I'm going to get him this time. He's going to be sorry he ever came after me."

Chapter 10

The determination that filled Kelly did not abandon her. Before Dean, she'd had more fire. She remembered it. If she looked back to the days before they met, she could easily remember a feistier Kelly. The feisty Kelly who had finally come to her rescue again when she at last accepted that there was no way to please Dean all the time. The Kelly who had the gumption to pack and leave.

The Kelly who had the gumption to stand in the muck of a canal and beat off an attacker.

"I like myself better now," she announced to Hank after a female deputy in civvies dropped off the beeper and receiver.

"What do you mean?" he asked.

"I'm going to deal with this instead of running. I ran from Dean, but I'm not running from this any longer."

"I'd hardly classify leaving an abusive husband as running. What were you going to do? Stay around and fight with him over and over until one of you was decked? That wasn't running. That was the only proper way to deal with him. The killer is a different thing and, honestly, I wouldn't blame you if you wanted to keep running."

"I'd blame myself. That's not me. Not the me I used to be before Dean."

He smiled. "I like you just the way you are."

"Well, running is not the way I am. Enough." She fingered the beeper that now hung around her neck on a chain. "I guess I need to stay here tonight. Alone."

"I guess so. But I'll be awake right next door."

"Thank you, Hank. Thank you for everything."

His brows rose. "Hold it right there. That sounds like a goodbye."

"I didn't mean it that way." Far from it. As she looked at him, she felt something approaching a craving to feel his arms around her again, his mouth against hers, his hands continuing the journey of exploration they had begun just last night.

Her heart must have been in her eyes, because he moved closer.

"Kelly?" His voice was quiet, husky.

"Yes?"

"Last night…I'm sorry about that."

A spark of hurt mixed with anger flared in her. "Sorry you kissed me and held me?" She heard the truculence of her own tone but couldn't call it back.

"No. Sorry I rolled away like that. I wouldn't blame you if you never wanted me to touch you again."

Her heart squeezed, an ache so sharp it surprised her with its force. *Too fast,* some little voice whispered. *Remember what happened with Dean.*

But she ignored that voice because if there was one thing

she was absolutely certain of it was this: Hank was nothing like Dean. Nothing.

Pain and yearning propelled her forward, and she slipped her arms around him, hugging him. To her vast relief, he hugged her back.

"Don't apologize," she said, her throat tight. "You couldn't help it. I didn't feel rejected."

"Thanks. Because it was certainly about the most offensive thing I could have done."

She felt awful for him. That he should consider a helpless reaction to terrible pain to be offensive... "No," she said firmly. "It wasn't offensive at all. I can't imagine that kind of pain, but I can sure understand why you needed to move."

She felt his big hand stroke her hair and for an instant she thought she could purr like a cat. It felt so good, she could hardly believe it. Had she ever felt that way with Dean? Probably. Maybe. But one thing for sure: She couldn't remember the last time she had felt like this.

She couldn't help but snuggle closer, needing to feel his warm strength, his male hardness everywhere. She wished he could just wrap right around her.

And with that came the unmistakable pulse of desire, but this time so strong it overpowered everything else in her mind. She wanted him. She didn't have room to spare for a thought about killers, or Dean, or the fact that her house had been invaded.

With an instinct so primal and so undeniable, she pressed her pelvis closer, sending a message as old as time. *I want you.*

She heard him catch his breath, and his arms tightened almost spasmodically around her. Then the world spun and she realized he had swept her off her feet. Dimly she was amazed that he could do that so easily after what he'd been through, but she liked the way it made her feel. She squeezed her eyes closed, trying to block out everything but the delightful sensations that now sparkled across her nerve endings, and the ache deep between her thighs that demanded an answer, and soon.

"Kelly."

Reluctantly, she opened her eyes and saw Hank looking down at her. He had a drowsy look that told her he was feeling the same things she was. Another spasm of need cramped between her legs.

"Are you sure?" he asked hoarsely.

Her answer came on a nearly breathless whisper, for all the air seemed to have vanished from the room. In fact, everything vanished except the arms that held her and the man who looked at her with sleepy hunger. "Yes…"

He had to turn sideways to get her through the kitchen door, down the short hall and into the bedroom, but it wasn't far and didn't seem to hurt him. She watched his face through heavy-lidded eyes, almost afraid that if she closed her eyes he would vanish.

He winced only once, as he bent to lay her down on the old bed. It wasn't as comfortable as the one she'd slept on at his place, but she was well past noticing that. At that moment the stone floor of a cave would have felt like heaven.

The merest brush of her own clothing seemed to strike sparks, and even the material of her pants, pressing between her legs, added to the flames. Never before had she realized just how erotic the whisper of her own clothing against her flesh could feel. The least movement fueled her hunger.

She felt herself opening, opening, like a plant eager for the sun's kiss. He tugged a foil packet from his jeans pocket and tossed it on the pillow. Then he moved cautiously to lay beside her and draw her carefully back into his embrace.

It was as if time stood still. The only thing that still existed, that still changed, was the syrupy heat that drizzled through her entire body. Arms around each other, they stared into one another's eyes, as if marking the exquisite importance of what was about to happen. As if any movement might dash the moment out of time.

Then he kissed her. Such simple words for such an explosion of feelings. The touch of his lips affected her as no one's ever had. Of that she was certain. No kiss had ever carried her so far, so fast, or stripped the last of her inhibitions away in an instant.

His did.

Over the past year, she had endured the death of most of her hopes, and all of her most cherished dreams. And then she had looked death in the eye. A deep change had occurred in her, one she did not realize until that instant: Everything good in life needed to be grabbed when it came by, because the chance might never come again. The only moment she could believe in anymore was right now. The future could hold almost anything. Much of her past lay in ashes. There was just now—this moment and this man.

She kissed him back, as much with passion for life as with passion for him, and then she pulled away, impatient with delays. Who knew how many hours or minutes she had left?

In an instant, everything within her shifted. She looked back at her struggles to perfect an impossible marriage, at a man who had tried to kill her over money, and realized that she had been struggling for some kind of future when the future might never happen.

Rising, she stood beside the bed and reached for his clothes. A surprised laugh escaped him, but he helped her yank away his shirt, his jeans, his shoes, his socks and briefs, until he lay naked.

Outside the storm finally reached them, booming hollowly,

and rain began to beat a tattoo on the roof. Inside another storm brewed: a hurricane of desire.

In the dim light, she could see hints of the scars that covered his body. Some appeared straight, surgical. Others spoke of tearing wounds. Patches of skin, shiny even in the half light, spoke of burns.

It had been even worse than he had told her.

Her throat tightened for him, but she could offer nothing to heal him, unless it was herself. She tugged at her own clothes, feeling bolder than she ever had in her life. Soon they lay at her feet, and she stood while he dragged his gaze over her. It affected her almost as strongly as a touch, and she stood proudly because the only damn thing about her that Dean had never criticized was her body. If she had confidence left in anything at all, it was that.

Then, slowly, she leaned over him and kissed him lightly. "Tell me," she said. "Tell me what pleases you and what doesn't hurt. We're going to do this your way because I want it to be as perfect as possible for you."

He said nothing for several seconds, eyes locked with hers. Then, "Straddle me."

But she didn't, not right away. Instead, she ran her palms over him from cheeks to belly, to hips to toe, savoring the texture of him, feeling her touches as if he touched her, too. No sex act in her life had ever come close to this, the feeling that she didn't know where she ended and he began. And all from touches.

His small nipples hardened, and she rubbed her palms over them, dragging a groan out of him. Then she kissed them, licking them as if they were her own. Another moan encouraged her.

Smiling with pleasure, she dragged her mouth lower, running her tongue down his center and then dragging it back and forth over his abdomen, feeling his muscles clench in response, feeling the shudders that tore through him.

His shaft was hard and she wrapped her hand around it. He jerked almost violently at the touch, and she felt the response in her grasp.

"You're beautiful," she told him. Then, driven by needs that were pulsing as hard and hot through her as they must be through him, she bent and ran her tongue along his staff.

"Kelly…"

She knew what he wanted. She wanted it, too. Her entire awareness seemed to be sinking to the place between her legs, so strong an ache it almost hurt. But she held back a little longer, clamping her thighs together as if that could help, and toying with him, enjoying the response she evoked.

Then he sabotaged her. Simply by reaching out and brushing his fingers over the nest of hair between her legs.

And electric shock caused her to catch her breath hard. Nor could she prevent it when his fingers demanded she loosen her legs for him. She gave him passage, and felt the gentlest of strokes on her petals, softening her, opening her even more until she stood bent over him, her legs apart, moans escaping her as he stroked and teased her petals apart, as his finger found its way into her hot depths.

"Hank…" She wanted this to go on forever, but she didn't know how much longer she could hold out. With every movement of his fingers, her legs weakened, her womanhood cried out for something deeper and harder.

"Ride me," he said roughly. "Now." He grabbed her hand and pressed the packet into it.

She rolled the protection onto him, enjoying the way he responded to her touch, wishing she could do without it because she liked his satiny skin better. But knowing he was right. Knowing this simple act cared for them both.

Then he tugged at her and she came to him as he asked,

placing her knees on either side of his hips, propping herself on her hands. "Fill me," she begged.

He reached down between them and guided himself into her. She closed her eyes as she felt him slip inside, stretching her and filling an emptiness she had forgotten she even had.

Then one of his hands found her breast, kneading it, his thumb torturing her nipple into exquisite awareness with every brush. With his other hand he found that tiny knot of nerves between her legs and rubbed it exactly right, as if he knew to the last degree what she needed.

Apparently, he did. Languorous movement began to speed up as demands took over from longing. There was only one place they wanted to go now, and their hips joined then separated a bit, a rocking motion as old as time.

The hard ache in Kelly grew until she was sure she couldn't stand it any longer. But the pinnacle remained just beyond her reach as she rode higher and higher.

Then it happened. An incredible hovering sensation, a feeling of tipping helpless on a precipice, uncertain whether she would make it over, or even if she could.

Moments later, stars exploded behind her eyelids. Her body clamped hard once more, then dissolved into throbbing waves of satisfaction.

She was dimly aware that he joined her seconds later.

Hank cradled Kelly on his chest, amazed by their love-making, warmed to his heart by the way she had chosen to take charge so that he wouldn't risk hurting any worse. Not all lovers were anywhere near so considerate.

He didn't doubt for a moment that she had been genuinely concerned for his pain. As he ran his hands down her damp back, feeling the last shivers of completion run through her, he wondered what in the world he had done to have a woman like this come into his life.

And right after he had decided to become a curmudgeonly hermit. Hah!

"Wow," she breathed.

"Definitely wow," he answered. Reluctantly, he moved her just enough to withdraw from his place within her before they could have an accident. She groaned a little, but helped him by moving to the side a bit.

She snuggled back in and he tightened his hold on her. The rain was pounding the roof right now, and he knew a moment of uneasiness. As loud as the storm was, they might not hear if someone tried to get into the house. Although it was still daylight, however dim, and that seemed an unlikely time to try a break in.

He wanted to stay right here, right now, indefinitely. He wanted to hold Kelly close, and soon make love to her again. But there was a creeping threat out there somewhere, and he couldn't give precedence to his wants over her needs.

She needed protection. He'd seen her reaction when she smelled that cologne—pure terror. He hoped he never saw that look on her face again, but he guessed he was going to, since she'd decided to stay here and face the threat.

Part of him felt a desperate urge to take her away, to carry her off to some safe place and then keep her with him every second until her court hearing was over. But he understood something else, and it was all that held him back: She needed to face and conquer this threat. She wasn't just tired of running. She was tired of the person it had turned her into. And from what little he had seen, Kelly Scanlon wasn't the type who hid from threats.

Running from Dean, as he had told her, was the only possible way to handle domestic abuse. You leave. But there were a lot of other things in life you didn't run from, and she wasn't a natural runner.

Realizing he had been silent for too long, remembering belatedly that women liked at least some pillow talk afterwards, he ran his hand over her hair and back and forced his thoughts back to right now and the gift that lay in his arms.

"Are you cold?" he asked. Dumb question, but they were lying there uncovered and she'd made no secret that she was a hot-weather girl.

"Not yet. I'm still warm." She stretched a little and lifted her head to smile at him. "That was wonderful. Thank you."

"I think I should thank you."

A little laugh escaped her, but it faded into a frown. "I guess we need to get dressed. That guy could come at any time."

"Most likely not until the middle of the night."

"Most likely, but it's easier to fight wearing clothes."

"True."

Reluctantly he let go of her, then lay there watching her gather up her clothes and dress. She finally turned to him with an impish smile as she pulled his sweatshirt around her. "Your turn."

Moving made him want to groan, but he stifled it. Not moving for much longer would only make it worse, so, much as he didn't want even two inches between them, he knew he had to get up.

She stood watching with a smile in her eyes as he dressed.

"You really are beautiful," she said.

"Me? No way. You're the beautiful one."

She shook her head. "You're beautiful in the ways that really count."

He heard some old pain there, and reached for her, drawing her close. "Kelly. So are you."

The smile that dawned on her face was like a rising sun on a clear morning. Too bad it didn't last.

Reality was a pain.

They went to the kitchen, still a mess and a long way from being the inviting place he wanted to make it, and she started coffee for them.

"Are you hungry?" she asked.

"Not really." No, dread had moved in, taking up residence in his stomach. He didn't like the thought that Kelly might have to face down her killer again, dependent only on a beeper around her neck and him watching from next door.

"There's got to be a better way to handle this," he said.

"What?"

"The guy coming after you. I don't want to be next door trying to see him approach through my windows. I don't want your life hanging by that beeper around your neck."

She leaned back against the counter and folded her arms. Her face became pinched. "I don't see how we can avoid it. If he sees that you're here, he won't come."

"And maybe that's just as well. I can accompany you back to Miami for the hearing. Then it'll stop regardless."

She shook her head. "No, Hank. That man attacked me. He tried to strangle me."

He watched her hand rise to her throat as if remembering.

"He hit me on the head and he tried to kill me," she went on, her voice quavering a bit. "I don't want him to get away with that. And if Dean was really behind it, and now it looks like he was or the guy wouldn't have followed me, then I don't want Dean to get away with it, either. What if some other young woman falls prey to his charm and then tries to leave him? Do you think he wouldn't do this again?"

"It's not your responsibility to protect hypothetical women."

"Maybe not. I don't know. Right now that's not my main concern. Right now I want those two creeps locked up for attempted murder."

He could scarcely argue with that feeling, although he was plenty worried about the means they were using. "There's still got to be a better way."

"If you think of one, I'll listen."

She turned and poured coffee for them both, then brought the mugs to the table.

"Maybe we can set up some traps for him," Hank said presently. "Something to make it hard for him to move through the house. To give you and everyone else time."

She cocked her head to one side. "Maybe. Any ideas?"

"Well, we've sure got enough debris in the living room. It doesn't have to be much. As it stands, he'll have to get in through the mudroom, because the new windows have burglarproof locks on them. So we know where he'll come from."

"Unless he picks the lock on the front door."

He frowned. "True. Okay, so we set up something there. It doesn't necessarily have to be something really noisy that might scare him off. But it needs to slow him down and let you know he's coming."

"I doubt I'll sleep at all."

"I know I won't. But he scoped the place out, obviously, and he has no reason to think we're going to move things around in here. Why would we? But what concerns me is that if this storm continues, you're not going to hear much if someone breaks in, and I'm not going to see much if I keep getting blinded by lightning flashes."

She nodded slowly. "I wasn't thinking of the storm."

As if to make sure she didn't forget it again, thunder cracked deafeningly.

Her eyes darted around nervously, and then she gave a little laugh. "Yup, that's going to be a problem if it keeps up."

"And he's got to be aware that the storm will help him, not hinder him. In theory, nobody's out and about, so any noise he makes will be drowned out."

"You're not making me feel any better."

"I'm not trying to. We can't afford to minimize any of this, overlook anything, make bad assumptions…"

"I get it," she said, cutting him off. "I'm not minimizing this. Believe me, I couldn't begin to. That man had his hands around my throat. I'll never forget how that felt."

He doubted she ever would. Maybe the point he was trying to make here didn't have anything to do with her minimizing the risk. Maybe it was simply that he didn't like the whole setup.

Rising from the table, he began to limp through the house, studying the place in a way he never had before, with an eye toward making Kelly safer.

Hell, he had absolutely no useful experience with this kind of thing. As a firefighter, he'd spent a lot of time making sure egresses were clear, not blocked. That people could get out, not that they couldn't get in.

"Crap," he said and turned to find that Kelly had followed him.

"What's wrong?"

"I have exactly the wrong kind of training for this. I clear paths, not block them."

"I would guess so." The fear that haunted her eyes softened a bit. "It's okay, Hank."

"No, it's not okay. If I can't stay with you because that might scare him off, then I'm damn well going to make sure he doesn't find you easy."

He went back down the hallway and looked at the piles of torn-up linoleum. The commercial trash collection bin he'd ordered still hadn't arrived, and maybe that was a good thing.

Loose linoleum could cause a minor trip, a skid. Something to delay the guy, cause him to make some noise. Staring at the pieces, an idea began to form.

"We don't want a major obstacle," he said. "Just something minor. To make him pause, or make a tiny bit of noise."

"Right." Kelly, too, was now looking at the ragged, bent linoleum as if she was following his train of thought.

"Let's go," he said. "Time to put back what we tore out."

It took over an hour, but pieces of linoleum soon covered the floor, dangerous now because the edges were bent upward. Not enough to trip, he judged, but enough to create a hindrance from time to time. They didn't slip much because he still hadn't begun to remove the layers of old adhesive, but those bent-up ends? Yeah, they'd catch his feet unexpectedly, even if he used a flashlight. It wasn't much.

"Now for the bedroom," he said.

"What about it?"

"Well, if he opens your bedroom door, we need some kind of noise to make him pause to alert you."

"But not too loud."

He nodded. "Exactly." Looking around, though, caused him pain. "This hurts."

"What does?"

"I've violated every principle I spent my life serving. If he can't get in here without tripping a bit, then you can't get out. I've built a trap for both of you."

She tilted her head to one side, taking in the scattered linoleum. "I didn't think about that part."

"I just did. I don't like this one bit."

"But I'll know to pick up my feet."

"What if you're in a hurry?" He just shook his head as lead settled in his stomach. The firefighter in him was rebelling, big-time. "It's why we're so insistent on fire codes and enforcing them. When people panic, when they need to run, even little obstacles can cost them their lives. This won't do."

"But what else is there?"

"I don't know. I just know we need to think some more." Then with a stifled groan, he started picking up the linoleum. Sometimes ideas weren't as good as they seemed at first. And this one was awful.

In fact, it was potentially deadly, even if no killer ever came.

He couldn't live with that.

Chapter 11

To Kelly's amazement, a short time later Hank came up with a truly masterful solution: wind chimes.

He reluctantly left her alone in the house, telling her to keep everything locked, and then fifteen minutes later returned with a box. When he opened it, it contained some glass wind chimes.

"I got them for my mother, but never had a chance to give them to her," he said. "They're not terribly loud, but probably loud enough to catch your attention, and very different from the storm sounds. If we hang them in the right spot, they should chime quietly if anyone opens a door or window."

"That's brilliant!"

"No, it's more like *Duh*. I can't believe we spent all that time building a firetrap."

Kelly laughed, even though, as the evening deepened, she felt more and more uneasy.

"Anyway," he went on, "I'll hold them up in various places,

you open a door or window, and we'll see if they chime. Then I want to test whether you can hear them in the bedroom."

"Okay."

The process took a while because he had to find exactly the right place where the intruder, whether he came from front or back, would stir the air enough to make the chimes sing quietly, and then make sure they were just loud enough for Kelly to hear in her bedroom. But finally a thumbtack pressed into the ceiling held them to one side in the kitchen doorway where their glass chimes made soft music easily when the air moved. Even walking down the hallway made them sing quietly.

"That's perfect," Kelly said. "I don't think it would scare him off, it's so quiet."

"But you can hear it through the closed door?"

"Faintly, but enough. You're right, it stands out from all the other sounds. It's very distinctive."

She had to admit that she felt better. Now she would have at least a little warning for sure. But she still wasn't happy about what she faced. Except for some time in the trunk when she'd evidently been unconscious, and a somewhat blurred memory of the first moments when she hit the water and realized what was happening, what she *did* remember was enough to make her adrenaline pump.

"I don't know whether he thought I was unconscious and would just drown," she told Hank now. "I can't remember parts of what happened very clearly because he hit me on the head. But I do remember rising up out of the water knowing I was going to die if I didn't get away."

"Do you remember fighting him?"

"Yes. Yes, I do. It's a blur, but I remember he was strong, I remember his hands squeezing my throat, and I remember he managed to dunk me a few more times because I couldn't get my purchase on anything with my feet. But once I did…" She trailed off, part of her wanting to erase the memory entirely, and part of her knowing she had to remember as much as she could so she knew exactly what she was up against.

"Adrenaline helped," she said finally. "I'm sure it did. And the self-defense classes I'd been taking. Once when he pushed me under I punched his groin."

"What finally got him to run?"

"I went for his eyes. But I also think he was as worried about alligators as I was. I mean, it was one thing to throw me off the bank. It was another to have to be in the water with me."

"That would make a difference, all right."

"He jumped in when I surfaced and gasped for air. I remember that. I think he thought he could finish me off fast. I mean, from what I can tell, I was unconscious until I hit the water. I only vaguely remember a little bit of the time I was in his trunk."

Hank nodded, clearly pondering what she was saying. "I don't think he's going to expect it to be quite as easy this time."

"Because I fought?"

"Like a wildcat evidently."

"So he'll be prepared for that this time." It almost sounded like a question, even though she meant it as a statement. In it she could hear her own rising level of fear. Her heart was beating faster now, and she felt queasy. It was going to happen again, maybe tonight, and this time he'd be expecting a fight. What if he came with a gun?

"He wanted to make it look like an accident last time," she said tentatively. "Wouldn't that be his goal now, too? Especially after I complained to the police that I thought Dean was trying to have me killed?"

"I can't read minds. But yeah, he might want to accomplish the same end."

"Then he might try to kidnap me again. Without leaving any signs here that he'd hurt me or that we'd fought."

He frowned. "You're not making me feel any better. What exactly are you thinking?"

"I'm not sure. There's no way to predict, anyway. It just occurred to me, when I thought that he might come with a gun, that he probably wouldn't do that. Links might be drawn back to Miami if it doesn't look like an accident."

"So you think he's going to try the same thing again?"

"At least insofar as getting me away from here to dispose of me."

"Then he's in for one hell of a surprise. No car is going to pull into your driveway in the middle of the night without being observed."

She nodded, wishing her stomach would stop sinking. But it had been sinking on and off since she smelled the cologne, and even more so as the day waned. Tonight, she thought. But at least it wouldn't come without warning.

Unlike last time. She shuddered a little, but Hank must have seen it. At once he tugged her close and hugged her tight. "We're going to get him," he said firmly.

"All I can say is, he'd better not keep me waiting too long. I'm sick of being scared."

And that was the absolute truth.

"I wish I could find a way to come back here tonight," he said. "If he's watching, though..."

"If he was smart enough to scope the place, he's smart enough to make sure I'm alone."

A lot of assumptions she thought, wishing she could just relax in Hank's arms and forget it all. Wishing the time they had spent together that afternoon was something she could be looking forward to repeating tonight. Wishing, always wishing.

"I've been wishing for things to get better for a long

time," she told him, her cheek pressed into the hollow of his shoulder. "It just suddenly struck me—I've been wishing my life away."

"Until you left Dean."

"Not really. I've been wishing the divorce was final for a while now, too."

"And now you want this night over."

"Yes. And I wish I could spend it with you instead of waiting for this guy."

He tightened his hold on her, and kissed her.

"Tomorrow night," he promised, as if there would be a tomorrow night. As if the killer would certainly fail. "Count on it."

She kissed him back, winding her arms around his neck, and ignoring all the voices reminding her that tomorrow could never be more than a promise. He was a man who rescued people. It was his nature. Their lovemaking, these kisses... they probably didn't mean a whole lot to him. He was a man after all, and men didn't feel the same way about these things that women did. Dean had sure taught her that.

But she was perfectly willing to indulge the illusion, for a short time. Because soon, all too soon, he'd pull back and she would know it was time to go.

Because he hadn't exactly seemed enthusiastic about her staying here. No. He seemed quite convinced that she was leaving. If anything, he'd done his best to make this sound like a boring place to live. So he probably felt it was safe to play her lover for a few days. And she would make certain it was, no matter how much it might hurt later.

They parted ways shortly after dinnertime. They stood out front while he made a show of telling her about the sod he wanted to lay and the garden he eventually intended to plant.

In case someone was watching. She couldn't imagine

where someone would hide and watch, except possibly in one of the two unoccupied houses on the street. Maybe he wasn't watching at all.

"I'm getting sick of trying to mind-read," she muttered as she pretended interest in the spot Hank was pointing to.

A snort escaped him. "Then quit. I think we've all anticipated as much as we can. Now it's up to him."

She stayed out front, watching as Hank limped back to his house. That limp looked painful tonight and she wondered if he was hurting badly or just exaggerating it for any observer.

Trying to read minds again, she thought, and turned to go back inside.

She paused, however, looking at the ramshackle house, the place she had rented only as a hideout. She didn't want to go back in there. She didn't want to be a rabbit waiting in a cage for its fate. Yet there was nothing else she could do.

The back of her neck began to prickle with awareness that he might be watching, even if she couldn't imagine from where. There were a couple of empty houses on the street. Would he hole up there?

Or would he just come back tonight and enter the house the way he probably had last night? Maybe he hadn't been there to scope out anything last night, but to kill her. If so, finding her gone would have frustrated him, but there were enough of her personal belongings scattered around to make it clear that she was staying here.

So he *would* come back.

With a deep breath, she forced herself to mount the steps and go back inside, then close and lock the door behind her. As long as he hadn't slipped in the back door while she and Hank were out front, everything was fine for now. Or so she told herself.

The wind chimes greeted her with their quiet music. She

had always loved wind chimes, and wondered if she would ever enjoy them again after this.

Uneasy, she walked through the house to ensure that she was alone. She checked the mudroom and found all the windows still locked and closed.

Not yet.

Then she forced herself to eat a can of soup, because she had to keep her strength up, even though it tasted like dust to her. And all the while she thought about Hank.

She kept trying to tell herself that she didn't know him very well, but as she sat there sipping soup from a spoon, she realized that she knew the important things: He'd stepped up to help a stranger, he'd risked his life to save someone else, and he had bought wind chimes for his mother. The three seemed to her to combine into the most sterling character references a man could have.

And not a single one of them was something Dean would have done. Heck, when he sent flowers for some occasion, his secretary always did it for him. Most of the time he knew about it only because his secretary reminded him that she had done it for him so he wouldn't suffer embarrassment by being surprised.

And after they married, the first few years, she had wondered if he had even chosen the jewelry he gave her for her birthday. Once he had stopped doing that, she had no doubt where those bouquets of roses came from. At first she had excused him; he was busy and didn't want to forget. But later she realized how meaningless it was to him: He couldn't be bothered to pick up the phone himself, or even stop at a florist's to place the order.

It wasn't as if he couldn't put reminders on his own computer calendar.

She suspected, however, that Hank had chosen those wind chimes for his mother himself. That he had taken the time to listen to a number of them, to look them over and to choose the set he thought would please her most.

He seemed like that kind of guy. A special kind of guy in so many ways.

Giving up at last on the soup, she dumped it and washed the dishes. The evening yawned before her, filled with unhappy and scary memories, and not nearly enough hope for the dawn.

Shortly after eleven, she turned out the last light, in her bedroom. She had spent the entire evening trying to read a book, staring at a single page without seeing it.

Now, in the dark, she felt as if her nerves had been stretched to the breaking point on a rack and she didn't know how much more she could stand.

But he would wait, she was sure, wanting to give her a chance to fall asleep. The last place he should find her was in her bed.

So she hunkered down in a corner of her bedroom, a hammer in hand, and waited. The storm had long since quieted, thank goodness, and the night seemed silent and still, except for the occasional car rolling past out front. She just hoped the air outside hadn't grown so still that when he opened a door or window there would be no breeze.

Then she recalled the way the wind chimes sounded when she just walked down the hall or through the kitchen door. It was quiet but distinct.

She would hear it. But even if she didn't she was in the wrong place. He'd seek her in her bed, and she wasn't there.

She fingered the beeper that hung around her neck, and imagined Hank next door, watching from darkened windows, keeping an eye out. Clinging to the image of him watching was her only real comfort just then.

How long would this take? What if he didn't come? If time still moved, it did so incredibly slowly.

Inevitably, she remembered that awful night in Miami, coming to full consciousness in the water, struggling against reeds, hardly able to tell up from down at first. Murky waters making it more difficult, desperate for air, and at last the flash of light that directed her upward.

Lungs near bursting, breaking the surface, gasping for air, more confused than she'd ever been in her life. Where was she? How had she gotten here?

Her head feeling almost split, like a melon, tasting the polluted water, full of oil from boat engines and God knew what else. Dragging air into burning lungs, the panic setting in hard as the pieces started to come together.

A glimpse of the canal bank, a glimpse of legs. Another lungful of air. A horrified word exploding in her brain: alligators.

She had to get out. She flailed at the water and the reeds, trying to reach the bank. Telling herself to calm down, she needed to think this all through in order to save herself, but her thoughts remained scattered and her heart was pounding hard. Panic kept driving her.

And then the awful splash nearby. At first she was sure it was an alligator coming for her...except, in some dim recess of her confused mind, she knew they didn't splash until they attacked.

The legs she had seen on the bank...surely someone would save her. But the legs were gone.

"Help," she croaked.

And that's when the hands closed around her throat. That's when she knew at a visceral level exactly what was happening.

The fight to get her feet on something, anything, for leverage. Going under again with hardly any air left. Some instinct rising in a tide of fury. She reached out to grab her attacker and felt hips. Moments later she punched him in the gonads.

The hands let go of her throat. She rose again swiftly, dragging in more air, looking wildly about until she saw the man coming at her again. Dim on the moonless night, lit only by light that still emanated from the houses that lined the canal, little enough at this hour. But she saw enough of his face, and enough of his determination, to know the fate he intended for her.

Then things blurred again. She remembered going for his eyes, determined to scratch them out. It was hard to move in the reeds and water, but now he faced the same hindrance.

He pushed her down again, and this time, her mind clearer, she grabbed at his belt for leverage and then punched him between the legs, harder this time.

She heard the howl even as she surfaced. He swiped at her, but then there was another splashing from up the canal. A gator? A person? No way to know.

As her attacker struggled to the bank, she lit into him again, holding on to him wherever she could and pounding him.

Alligators preferred to hunt in the evening or at night, and the splashing she and her attacker made would be inviting to any gator. The thought ratcheted up her already-screaming terror.

The guy reached the bank. By now she was hanging on to his back and pummeling him with everything she had. Neither of them would get out of this canal at this rate.

Some primal instinct made her let go and reach for the canal's cement wall herself. Before she could pull herself out, her attacker had already done so and taken off running.

As she levered herself onto the bank, she heard a car start, then watched with dazed eyes as it drove away without even turning on the lights.

At that point, all she knew was that she had to get far enough away from the water that a gator couldn't leap out and grab her.

She crawled, her head throbbing as if a hammer beat on it. Across grass, across gravel, toward a porch. Toward a worried voice that must have heard something and called out. Toward a flashlight beam that steadily moved toward her.

She shook herself now, as she sat in the corner of her darkened bedroom. That was then, she reminded herself. This was now, and this time she wouldn't be fighting water and reeds. This time she would be ready. And this time she would make him truly sorry.

From various windows in his house, Hank kept watch, ignoring the grinding pain in his hip, the constant ache in his back, the random pains that shot through bones that would never, it seemed, forget that they had been shattered and pinned together.

The pain, though, was a dull background to the worry that gnawed at him. He respected Kelly's wish to end this as quickly as possible. He respected her courage in deciding to stay alone in her house. He respected her decision not to run again.

Hell, he just plain respected her. For all she was inclined to put herself down because of perceived past failings, all he could see was a remarkably strong young woman. Being wrong about a guy like Dean was a mistake made by millions. Having the guts to get out after eight years of abuse that had certainly undercut her confidence was not something everyone possessed. As a fireman, he'd been called to many domestic violence scenes because EMTs were needed. He'd looked at women, and sometimes men, who'd been battered to within an inch of their lives. He'd seen the terror in their eyes, and he'd seen the violence in their attackers.

So many couldn't leave because they were terrified of what would happen if they did. Many stayed because they had been taught to believe they deserved it.

Somehow Kelly had preserved a basic strength of character through all that—something that not everyone could. And now she was ready to face a killer in the dark and alone.

Hell, she was amazing.

It went against all his instincts and all his training not to just barge on over there, toss her over his shoulder and carry her to safety.

He knew Gage would have his deputies nearby. That they, too, expected the attack tonight. He imagined them circling the area in unmarked cars, waiting for her to hit the button on her beeper, trying not to get too close or be too obvious, while still not drifting too far away.

The thought didn't comfort him much. In just a few short days, Kelly had come to mean considerably more to him than just a damsel in distress who needed some help. Far more.

How much more he really didn't want to consider, because he was sure, absolutely sure, that this tiny town couldn't hold her for long. He no longer felt the need for excitement, and his body would no longer allow him to risk his neck to save others. What he loved here were his roots, and the quiet life after the frenzy of being a big-city firefighter. He'd had all the excitement he wanted, and now he was happy to get together with friends, old and new. His idea of a great Friday night was hanging out at Mahoney's, or going out to dinner with Mike Windwalker and his new wife, or dropping in on Gage and Emma Dalton.

Not a whole lot of excitement when he considered the array of delights offered by a large city like Miami. And Kelly had obviously lived in the fast lane during her marriage.

So how could he—or this place—begin to compete?

But why should he even ponder such things? She hadn't pledged her troth to him; she'd simply made love with him. That wasn't a promise of any kind. She had probably succumbed not only to desire, but to a need to forget for a little while.

He'd be stupid to look at it as anything else.

Just as 2:00 a.m. approached, and a yawn was trying to crack his jaws, he thought he caught sight of movement behind Kelly's house. The storm had blown away, but clouds still rendered the night darker than usual. He strained his eyes, wondering if he had imagined it. Tree limbs were still tossing a bit, and an errant light could have created a shadow. He didn't want to show himself too soon in case the guy hadn't moved in yet. Scaring him away would only prolong Kelly's hell.

Every muscle in his body tensed as he strained to see. Where was it?

From time to time, Kelly had to stand up and stretch her stiffening muscles. When she did so, she tried to move as quietly as possible, for fear of not hearing the intruder, or of warning him that she was awake.

She was almost afraid to pull up her sleeve and look at her watch, but reminded herself that her bedroom door hadn't opened yet. Even if someone was in the house, he couldn't possibly see the faint glow from the dial.

A few minutes past two. She leaned back against the wall, shaking her legs to restore circulation, then did a deep-knee bend. If time could move any slower, she didn't know how.

Come on, she thought. *Come on, let's just get it over with.*

While she may have wished time away in the past, never had she wished it gone as much as she did now. Waiting had never suited her well, but tonight it didn't suit her at all. As the minutes crept by, she worried that dread was keeping her at a high pitch too long, that at some point weariness would overtake her, slow her down, make her less alert. Surely she couldn't stay this wound up forever.

But almost as soon as she wondered about it, adrenaline taught her a lesson: It had an even higher gear.

She thought she heard something. Not the wind chimes. But something. Was it a tree rustling outdoors, or brushing the house? She wasn't sure, and she hadn't spent enough time in this house to recognize its normal night noises.

Something had caught her attention. All she could do was tighten her grip on the hammer and wait, straining her ears. A lifetime seemed to pass in the next couple of minutes.

Then again, another sound. A crunch? She wished she could be sure. What would be crunching? She tried to remember the sounds the house made as she walked through. Maybe some of the crumbling glue from the floor?

Tensing until her muscles started to ache, she waited. No amount of effort could get her to relax, and she feared cramping at the wrong time. She shook her arms, tried to stretch her legs.

Then she heard the faint clink of the wind chimes.

Or had she?

Damn, it hadn't sounded so faint earlier. Was she imagining it? She fingered the beeper hanging around her neck and wondered if she should use it.

One thought and one thought alone held her back. If she was wrong, if she'd imagined that faint sound of wind chimes and the police descended on this place, she'd be back to her endless game of cat and mouse with a killer. She'd have no idea when she might be at risk, or when she might be safe.

She'd have to pack up and leave again because he wouldn't attack her here at the house once more, not after a rapid police response. So he'd be out there somewhere, basically making her a prisoner in this house until she went somewhere by herself.

So she'd have to go on the run again or accept being a prisoner for the next two months. Both thoughts sickened her, but what sickened her most of all was the thought of leaving Hank behind.

Oh, God! What had she done? Fallen in love in a matter of days? Was she an idiot? Hadn't she learned anything about caution, and getting to know someone before throwing her cap over the moon?

Apparently not. And yet, she had thought she knew Dean. She'd worked for him. They'd dated for months before she accepted his proposal. Yes, she had thought she'd known him, and in the end it had turned out that she didn't know the most important things about him.

Maybe she didn't know Hank, but she knew the important things about *him.* At this very moment he was next door, waiting to run to her rescue. From the moment he'd met her, he'd put himself out in all sorts of ways to take care of her. Dean had never done that.

Hell, Dean had snowed her. Flattered her. Swept her away. But, in retrospect, she tried to remember a single time, just one time, when he'd put himself out a tiny little bit just for her.

And she couldn't.

The fear that held her hostage, that turned her muscles into tightly wound wires, suddenly gave way to a blinding rage. Adrenaline flooded her, and she made up her mind that this was it. Tonight. She hefted the hammer and waited. It would end here.

Then she heard it. No mistaking it this time. The wind chimes. Drawing a deep breath, she pressed the beeper button.

He didn't even have to try to kill her, she reminded herself. Just the fact that he was in her house would be enough to get him put away. And maybe enough to get Dean.

Maybe.

Both hands grasped the hammer shaft now, and her eyes remained fixed on her bedroom door. But it didn't open.

What…?

Hank heard the beeper in his pocket go off. In a flash, as if he weren't a sack of screaming bones and muscles, he dashed for his back door and outside. In the distance he could hear the approach of multiple car engines: the deputies.

He wasn't about to wait for them. Kelly could be dead by the time they arrived.

He got to the back of her house and found the window open. He wasted a split second on deciding whether to climb through or use his key on the back door, a mental measurement of what would be faster. And more practical, because damn, hanging half in and out that open window…

He headed for the back door and was almost there when it burst open and a dark shadow hurtled out of it. At once he leapt, but his hip chose that moment to fail him, and he barely clasped a shoe before he hit the ground on his stomach and the shadow vanished into the night.

Dammit!

He tried to scramble to his feet, ignoring his disobedient body, just as other shadows rounded the house. Silently, he pointed them in the direction the man had fled. Two deputies split up. Guns in hand they took off at a speed he could only envy.

Then another deputy came and dashed into the house.

Reaching his feet at last, Hank stumbled after him, scared to death. He threw on lights as they went and at last they reached the door of Kelly's room.

"He's gone," Hank told Jared Locke. "Unless there's more than one of them."

Locke nodded, standing to one side of the door, his weapon in both hands. "Call her."

"Kelly? Kelly are you okay?"

The door burst open and he saw Kelly standing there, hammer in her hand, her eyes almost wild. "He ran," she said, her voice shaking. "Why the hell did he run?"

Hank tore his gaze from her and looked down the short hall. The wind chimes sang merrily.

"Hell," he said. "Oh, hell."

Chapter 12

"There's nothing," Hank said angrily, "quite like outsmarting yourself."

They were gathered in his living room—Kelly, Gage, Jared Locke and the two deputies who had failed to find the intruder. "Dammit, it never occurred to me that he'd take those wind chimes as anything except an addition to the house."

"He's smart," Gage said. "Smarter than I hoped. He must have realized the sound could have warned Kelly, that maybe she'd put the chimes there to do just that."

"So what now?" Kelly asked.

Hank looked at her and ached. Her eyes were smudged, dark circles of fear and stress, making her look hollow.

"What now?" she asked again.

None of them answered, and Hank hated it. They'd used her as bait. It wasn't going to work a second time. Now she'd be at risk anywhere, anytime and they couldn't shadow her every second. None of them except him, that was.

"You're moving in here," he said. "You're not going to be alone again."

"I can't ask that."

"You're not asking anything," he said forcefully. "I'm offering. In fact, I'm demanding. He's going to try again and he's going to have to deal with both of us. And after tonight he probably figures I'm no problem at all."

The bitterness with which he spoke the words shocked him. He closed his eyes, reaching for some self-control, some clear thinking beside the horrible helplessness he felt, the failure he felt because his hip had given out.

"Oh, hell," he said finally. "Who am I kidding? I couldn't even get across the yard without collapsing. Maybe we need to get you a permanent private security escort."

"I can't afford that and I don't want it," Kelly said. Her voice grew stronger. "Don't beat yourself up, Hank."

"Why not? The wind chimes were my brilliant idea. Then I almost had the guy and my leg gave out. Some protector I am."

"Stop it," Kelly said angrily. "Please stop it. Nobody thought the guy was going to run like that. Even the deputies couldn't catch him."

"Yeah, but he had a head start on *them*."

Silence filled the room. Gage rubbed his chin finally and sighed. "Okay, what do we know? We know the guy is for real, he broke in twice, he was smart enough to get scared off by wind chimes. That means he's going to look for another time and place. That means Kelly can't be alone. I can arrange a loose watch, but there's no way I can staple a deputy to her side. That leaves you, Hank."

"Yeah, no reason he should fear me," Hank said harshly.

"And that's where he's wrong," Gage said firmly. "He's absolutely wrong. And that's going to be his mistake."

Hank stared at him from burning eyes. "He's not wrong, Gage."

"Yes, he is. First off, what happened tonight could have happened to anyone and he was already running. What if he hadn't been running? What if you'd cornered him in the house? I think you'd have given him a whole lot more trouble."

"Maybe." He'd allow that much, not much more.

"My feeling is that if Kelly stays with you, he'll try again. He'll come prepared to deal with a woman and a cripple."

"Don't say that," Kelly snapped. "Hank's not a cripple."

"No, he's not. But that's something the perp isn't going to know. Hell, anyone who sees Hank limping around and doesn't know him is bound to underestimate him."

"Especially after I wound up on my face making a simple tackle."

"That'll work *for* us," Gage said firmly. He looked at Kelly. "What do you think?"

"About what? Whether I'll feel safe with Hank? Of course I will. Safer than I will anywhere else, that's for sure."

That was almost an indictment, Hank thought miserably. *Safer than anywhere else.* He counted more than no one. That thought pierced him to the core.

Kelly rose from the rocker where she had been sitting, and crossed the room to his side. "That came out wrong," she said.

"It's okay. It's true."

"It's not true." She laid her hand on his arm and he forced himself to look at her. What he saw in her blue eyes was concern and warmth.

"It *is* true. You're a born protector, Hank. It shows in everything you do. I trust you with my life."

That could be a mistake, he thought with uncharacteristic bitterness. He'd failed again tonight, the same way he'd failed his friends in a burning building.

But he couldn't argue. He knew Gage was right about not being able to staple a deputy to her side. He simply didn't have the manpower, and even if he did, they'd never catch the guy. And Kelly wanted him caught. She wanted him to pay for trying to kill her, and if Dean was behind it, she wanted Dean to pay, too.

He could understand that need, and while turning the other cheek was his usual rule of life, that didn't feel quite right when it came to murder or attempted murder.

There were times when you failed society by not pursuing justice.

"Okay," he said after a moment. "I'll do my damnedest."

"Keep the beeper," Gage said, standing. "But I'm going to have to loosen the cordon more now that he's probably had a chance to see how fast we responded. I'll make it look like we think the threat is over."

"Maybe it is," Kelly said. But she didn't look or sound as if she believed it.

"I doubt it," Gage said frankly. "But I want him to think what happened tonight was our usual response to an emergency call, and that we think it was a random break-in and we're not convinced anything more will happen. That perception will be enhanced by your moving over here. You can appear frightened, but we need to look as if we think nothing's going to happen. Make him feel secure enough to try again."

He paused. "It probably won't happen tonight, although I suppose it could. It depends on whether he thinks you won't be expecting another break-in so soon. He must figure you know someone's after you, because you ran, and you accused your husband of trying to have you killed. But whether he suspects you know he's here will have a huge impact on his decision making, and I have no idea whether he does or not. Just stay on your toes."

At last everyone left, just as the advent of dawn was lightening the night a bit.

"I think we could both use some sleep," Hank suggested.

Kelly nodded, still looking hollow. "Where do you want me to sleep?"

"With me, of course. I'm not letting you out of my sight."

Nor did he want to. If there was one thing he had learned in the past few hours, it was that having her out of sight right now created a deep anxiety in him. He wasn't volunteering for any more of that.

Later while Kelly slept deeply, he lay awake staring at a ceiling that brightened steadily, even though the curtains were drawn. He'd come up hard tonight against limitations he'd been refusing to accept for some time. Yeah, he could ignore the pain and do almost everything he needed to, and a lot of what he wanted to, but he couldn't do anything at all when his hip just quit like that.

What if he failed her the way he'd failed Fran and Allan?

If he couldn't protect her, what earthly use was he? Just another person taking up space and using up air, that's all.

But even as he had that self-pitying thought, he kicked himself mentally. *Dis*abled did not mean *un*able. There might be things he could no longer do, but choosing a metric like this would doom him to be one of those people he'd always loathed—the kind of people who sat around complaining about relatively little because they had a problem of some kind.

The odd thing was, the truly disabled people he'd met over

the years had been the ones who usually complained least about everything. He'd decided after his accident to use them as an example and not let himself sink into the pits.

Okay, he'd launched himself and discovered that his hip was no longer able to do that. So he'd have to come up with other ways of achieving the same end…if he ever needed to do it again. God willing he wouldn't.

As for the rest, he had to keep reminding himself that he wasn't doing that badly. He could still be a cowboy when he felt like taking the work, he could still remodel houses, still indulge his passion for carpentry when he chose. He was far from crippled.

That word had stung, though he knew why Gage had used it. And Gage, who wasn't a whole lot better off than he was, certainly hadn't meant it the way it had struck him. He'd only meant that whoever was after Kelly would see it that way.

And that was a good thing, right?

He dozed finally, the way he had often dozed at the firehouse, filling in quiet moments with needed sleep, but a sleep light enough to wake at a single unfamiliar sound.

Kelly woke in the late morning tangled all around Hank. His presence had made it possible for her to sink deeper into sleep than she had in a while, and she felt refreshed.

When she opened her eyes, she saw his face inches away. He was sleeping, his breathing deep and steady. She didn't want to disturb him, so she indulged herself in the opportunity to drink in every detail of his features. When it came to a man, that was something she hadn't wanted to do in a very long time, and she felt a little silly for doing it. That was the kind of thing she'd done in high school. And briefly with Dean, but not since.

Hank was relaxed now, more relaxed than she'd seen him before, and she admired the strong lines of his face, the mouth that had given her so much pleasure. She longed to reach out and touch him. Right now he probably didn't hurt, and that alone would have made her let him sleep forever.

Remembering how down he had been on himself earlier when he had failed to capture the man who was running from her house, she ached. She wished she could find a way to reassure him that it didn't matter, not in any real sense. What mattered far more was the kind of man he was, all the countless things he did to make her feel better and safer. A lot of people could probably make a flying tackle, and a lot more probably couldn't. But the world wasn't exactly overflowing with people who would upend their lives for a stranger.

And even fewer, she was sure, who were such considerate lovers. Such incredible lovers. She realized that she didn't have a huge sample set, but Dean had been a selfish lover. Maybe not as bad as some—how would she know?—but she knew enough to realize that Hank was pretty special.

Now, even after his self-disappointment last night he was prepared to put it all on the line again to keep her safe.

She had done nothing at all to deserve that from him. To earn it. It spoke eloquently to his character.

And she was going to miss him like hell. It was almost worth waiting here for a murderer to strike again just so she could spend these moments lying beside him.

Or maybe it *was* worth it. All of it. Everything that had brought her to this moment and this place.

Because her life would have been a whole lot poorer if she had never met Hank Jackson, and it would be immeasurably poorer when she left.

If only he had evinced a desire, a mere wish, for her to stay when this was over. But he hadn't, not once. Nor could she imagine why he would even suggest it. He hadn't exactly overwhelmed her with his description of this town, and she often got the feeling that he viewed her as a city girl and himself as a mere cowboy. As if they had nothing in common and never would.

She sighed, quietly she thought, but it was enough to make Hank's eyes snap open.

"You okay?" he asked. He didn't sound at all sleepy or groggy. Amazing.

"Sorry, I'm fine. I didn't mean to disturb you."

"Don't worry about it. I've been sleeping with my ears open."

She wanted to sink into his embrace, to make love, to pretend that everything was fine, the day glorious, and maybe even imagine the man beside her cared about her in ways beyond keeping her alive.

But that didn't happen. He lifted his free arm, glanced at his watch.

"Time," he said.

"Time for what?"

"Time to shower, to eat, to get ready." He gave her a quick squeeze with one arm, then disentangled himself from her, leaving her feeling bereft.

"What's the rush?" she asked almost irritably.

He glanced over his shoulder. "I'm not going to fall on my face this time."

She snapped up into a sitting position. "Stop it, Hank. Just stop it."

"Why? It's true. I have to compensate. I'm not the guy I used to be."

"Has it occurred to you that maybe you're a *better* guy now?" She jumped out of bed, grabbing for her duffel, planning to shower and change.

"What the hell is that supposed to mean?" he demanded. "I'm all busted up. I couldn't make a single freaking tackle last night, something I used to be able to do without even thinking about it."

"So?"

"So?"

"Yeah, so?" She faced him, angry and not even sure why, except that reality was screwing up things again, and she couldn't stand to hear him put himself down. Angry because they should be making love like ordinary people instead of leaping out of bed because some killer wanted another swipe at her.

Hell, she was just *angry*.

"What did I miss?" he asked, apparently getting a little angry, too. "Some part of your personal mental conversation I'm not privy to? I screwed up last night. I'd be an idiot to ignore my limitations again. What's your problem with that?"

"I hate to hear you put yourself down. You fell. Anyone could fall."

"Not because their hip gave out."

"Big deal. A million people could have had a knee give out. Or could have tripped on something. When did perfection become your personal standard for worth?"

He opened his mouth, but then snapped it closed. "Watch it," he said quietly.

"Why? I'm beginning to wonder if the only thing you care about is making up for what happened to your friends. Well, if that's what you need, Hank Jackson, you're going to be sorely disappointed. I can take care of myself!"

She was almost out the door when the cruelty of what she had just said hit her. Instantly, she felt the blood drain from her head, and she swayed, grabbing the door frame. "Hank, I'm sorry."

"Too late," he said harshly. "You can take your pop psychology and shove it. If I made any mistake, it was thinking that I could actually help you out."

Then he shoved through the door beside her and disappeared

into the kitchen. He didn't leave the house, but considering how he'd left her feeling, he might as well have.

She had thought she knew loneliness. But nothing in her life had prepared her for the loneliness Hank left in his wake.

He slammed pans around in the kitchen, only because he wasn't the type to punch a hole in the wall, much as he felt like it.

Yeah, he felt like a failure after that missed tackle last night. Yeah, it had reminded him of Fran and Allan, although he knew perfectly well that the circumstances had been different. Hell, he'd been through enough therapy after that to have a thoroughly shrunken head. His hang-ups had all been hung out to dry, and, in the process, most had disappeared. He still grieved, he still felt bad, and survivor guilt might dog him forever, but he wasn't walking around looking for a bandage to put on the wound anymore.

And for her to accuse him of that made him madder than a hornet. All he was doing was recognizing his physical limitations. That was realistic, not neurotic.

When he had banged the pots enough to realize that it wasn't giving him any more satisfaction, he set about making a hearty meal. If there was one thing he knew from his years as a firefighter, it was that you couldn't afford to let your energy level ebb. Not ever. And if that meant eating when you were angry, or upset, or just not hungry, sometimes you had to do it, because that call would come and running out without sufficient fuel in your system made you a whole lot less effective.

He made home fries from scratch. He made a mound of scrambled eggs seasoned with green pepper and onions, he pulled a gallon of orange juice from the refrigerator. It cast him back to his days at the firehouse, and gradually his mood improved. He knew he'd made more food than the two of them could possibly eat, but he didn't care. Cooking for a horde, even one that wasn't there, had always put him in a better frame of mind.

"That's a lot of food," Kelly said quietly.

He turned from the table to see her standing in the kitchen doorway, her hair still damp, her duffel over her shoulder.

"You're not leaving," he said.

"I should. I said something unforgivable."

"We're on edge. We may say other things before this is over."

"I'm still sorry. I don't know where that came from."

He regarded her, at once sad and weary. "The only question I have is this: Did you believe it? Do you believe it?"

"No." She shook her head, and a tear rolled down her cheek, making him feel like an ogre. "I was angry. I'm just so angry about this mess. My whole life is crumbling because my ex wants me dead, and I missed the chance to end it last night because the guy he sent after me evidently has a brain. So now I don't know how long it will be, or how much more of this…" Her voice broke. "And I hate to hear you put yourself down. When I said that…I was just trying to say you shouldn't be so hard on yourself, and that was the most extreme thing that popped into my head so you'd stop."

He could see that, he supposed. She probably read his honest assessment of his limitations as self-pity, and she'd chose something cutting to say to shake him out of it. And being angry…well, he knew all about that, he supposed. He could still wince when he remembered some of the things he'd said in anger after the building collapse. "Okay," he said. "Let's forget it. And you have to eat. Want to or not, it's important. This wouldn't be a good time to run out of energy."

"No." But she still didn't move.

"Dammit, Kelly, you're not leaving. If you do, I'm going to be right on your heels. So just drop that dang bag and get in here and eat before it all turns cold."

The duffel slid slowly to the floor, and looking almost like a chastised kid, she came to sit at the table. He started heaping food on her plate. "Eat as much as you can. I won't make you clean your plate."

Then he filled his own and sat facing her. He waited until she picked up her fork and speared a potato.

"I'll tell you something," he said after a moment. "I had a good year of therapy after the accident. I don't have a whole lot of hang-ups left. I sure as hell have nothing to prove. I just want to keep you safe. And to do that, I have to recognize my limitations."

"I'm sorry."

"Don't apologize again. You don't need to do it, and I don't need to hear it. We all say things we regret later, and half the time we don't even know why we said them. You didn't commit a mortal sin, and I'm over it, okay?"

"Okay." She ate another potato.

"In fact," he said a little while later, "I'm actually glad you got mad at me."

Her head jerked up and she stared at him from wide blue eyes. "You're kidding, right?"

"Nope. Because if there's one thing that's clear to me now, it's that Dean didn't cow you. Not one little bit."

At that, a tiny smile crept into the corners of her mouth, lifting them.

He felt his own heart lift at the sight. More than it should have. Warning bells tried to sound in his head, telling him he was getting too deeply involved, but he ignored them.

Life would deal the deck as life chose. If there was one thing he'd finally learned, it was that very little was controllable. The good and the bad just happened. And when it came to people, there was no hedge against the pain. It either happened or it didn't.

"I need to go back to my place," Kelly said that evening. They'd spent what was left of the afternoon playing cards, holding hands and gazing into one another's eyes a little more than they probably should have. The smoke of desire had been wafting around them the whole time, but evidently neither of them wanted to give in to it just then. Maybe because they were both too tense, and neither of them could fully relax.

Hank looked at her. "Why?"

"Because he won't come after me when he thinks someone else is around."

"Gage thinks he'll count me out."

"I don't count you out. Why should he?"

He could think of plenty of reasons, including his falling flat on his face last night. But he decided not to argue, even though his stomach had just done a flip, and her decision was about to give him an acute anxiety attack.

"I need this to be over," she said again. "I *need* it to be done. I can't keep this up. So I'm going back. I'm giving him his chance. And this time I won't be waiting in the bedroom."

"Look," he said, "he already suspects something because of the wind chimes and the quick police response. There's no reason to think he'll go back there now. He's more likely to come here."

"How do you figure that?"

"Because if I were him I'd assume you heard him break in, that you called 9-1-1, and there was a fast response because this is a small town. And if you stay here tonight, he's likely to think your guard is completely down because you're not alone."

He watched her think about that, glad that she was thinking it through, not arguing from impulse.

"This is getting beyond enough," she said finally. "I'll never be rid of him unless we catch him. But you can't follow me everywhere any more than a cop can. We've got to give him an opening and hope he takes it."

This whole situation began to strike him as impossible, but he didn't say that out loud. It would serve no purpose.

"Okay," he said finally. "I'll walk you home later. Much later. I'll leave you on the front porch. And then I'll head out like I'm going to take a walk. I'll look as lame as I can manage."

She surprised him with a little laugh. "Like a bird pretending to have a broken wing to protect her nest."

"It works for birds." He responded with a smile of his own, even though he was feeling sicker by the minute at the risk she was proposing. But she was right. They had to give the guy his opportunity, or live like this indefinitely.

"Just don't lock your doors," he said. "If I have to fumble with a key, last night is going to look like a ballet."

She laughed genuinely then, and the sound lifted his heart. "I guess you'd better let Gage know or he'll come to the wrong house when I hit the beeper."

"And just so you know, I'm not going to be that far away. It's going to look like I'm out for a long walk—maybe to Mahoney's bar—but I'll be skulking in backyards as long as I don't get arrested." His tone brooked no argument.

Once again he had to hand it to her for guts. He just didn't know if his own gut could stand it.

It was past eleven when they stood on her porch. The night had quieted down—few folks were stirring. They had planned this conversation, and he hoped it sounded natural.

"Are you sure you don't want to come to Mahoney's with

me?" he asked, just loudly enough to ensure that his voice carried.

"Sorry, Hank, I'm exhausted from last night. I just need to sleep. But thanks anyway."

"Sure."

He bent to kiss her lightly, murmuring for her to be careful, then hobbled down the steps, trying to make it look as if he'd hurt himself more last night.

"Take your truck," she called after him.

"Nah. I need to work out the kinks. The walk will do me good." He gave a little wave and headed down the street.

It all looked perfectly natural, including his exaggerated limp. Difficult though it was not to look back, he kept walking, but his neck prickled with the certainty that someone was watching.

He rounded the corner at last, walked halfway down the block, then started his cut back through neighbors' yards, taking care not to pass anywhere near the Calvins' yard where their dog would start barking.

But the guy had to have figured out about the dog, too, in his recon. So he'd be coming from the other direction, right?

So Hank hoped. As soon as he hit the shadows, he slowed down and moved with every bit of stealth he could muster. It wouldn't do to scare the guy off again.

Kelly stood on the porch for a while, watching Hank walk away, then pretending to take in the night's quiet. Inside, she was a taut bundle of nerves, but she wanted to do everything possible to make it look as if she believed last night had just been a random break-in. There was no reason on earth for the guy to think she knew he had followed her. Not with the Miami PD claiming his first attack had been a mugging. Not when she'd been on the run for weeks.

She was betting her life tonight that he believed she felt reasonably safe.

The thought caused a chill to run through her, but she suppressed the shiver. It *was* getting cold out here, though. In Miami, the water kept the difference between day and night temperatures minimal. Here, when the sun went down, there was little to hang onto the day's heat.

Finally, deciding she had looked relaxed enough, or at least she had done so as long as she possibly could, she went inside.

She flipped on a few lights, trying to act as she would any evening. A stop in the kitchen for water, a quick trip to the bathroom. Then, switching off lights behind her, she went to the bedroom, where she bunched up pillows under the covers. The hammer was still there, lying on the floor. She picked it up and put it on the bed. Watching the clock, she forced herself to wait twenty minutes before she turned off the light as if she were going to sleep.

It was the quietest night yet here. She worried that that might put him off.

But almost in answer to her thoughts, she heard a breeze kick up. The house creaked a little, the leaves outside rustled. Good.

And once again she took up her station in the corner near the door. He would expect her to be in bed. The element of surprise would help her.

She told herself every positive thing she could think of, trying to hold off the tension and anxiety as long as possible. He'd wait a while, until he felt reasonably certain that she was asleep. But this time he would know to avoid the wind chimes.

Front door, she decided. It was the only way for him to come in without walking through the kitchen.

The only way that would minimize the sounds the chimes made.

God, time crept by.

Then she heard it. The unmistakable tinkle of the wind chimes. Faint. Barely audible. She nearly held her breath, hoping that this time he wouldn't be scared off. Man, he must be as tired of this cat-and-mouse game as she was.

Then nothing. Absolute silence except for the sighing of the breeze in the trees. He was waiting, she was sure. Waiting to see if there was any reaction to the chimes.

Maybe they hadn't been what scared him off last night. Maybe something else had made him take flight. Maybe he'd heard her move in her bedroom. Because she had. She remembered standing up, getting ready. Or maybe he'd heard Hank come barreling out of his house.

Thinking about it now, she was sure that must have been it, and not the chimes at all. They were so quiet. But when she'd heard them last night, she'd pressed the beeper and Hank had come running out…and she suspected he hadn't been trying to be quiet.

Tonight there would be no sound from Hank's house. No sound of a door opening, no sound of hurried, limping footsteps on his back stoop. No other warning but the wind chimes.

The quiet minutes dragged. She fingered the beeper but refused to push it yet. She had to be sure because if he escaped again she was almost certain he wouldn't try once more here. No, he'd wait for a moment when she was out somewhere by herself, and sooner or later she was going to have to walk to the store or something. Because she couldn't stay locked in forever, and Hank couldn't possibly be there every moment.

So it had to be tonight.

Twenty minutes passed. She had just about made up her

mind that she'd imagined the sounds when she heard a quiet, creeping step outside. He was moving through the house cautiously, carefully, as silently as he could.

At least he probably didn't have a gun, she told herself. A gunshot would wake the whole neighborhood. A shooting death would open inquiries that would stretch all the way back to Miami once her identity was known because they would check into her past. So what did he plan to do?

Thoughts of chloroform filled her mind. He could knock her out and then suffocate her. But no, if he wanted this to look as if it had just been a simple break-in gone awry, it would be better if he hit her with something. Beat her to death.

She gripped the hammer more tightly and felt for the beeper.

The faintest of crackles, right outside her door. Then it began to swing inward. She pressed the beeper button.

Hank felt the beeper go off in his pocket. He was three houses down now, although at that moment it looked like he was miles away. And somehow in his gut he knew Kelly had waited until the last minute.

He took off with a speed he'd almost forgotten he had, giving no thought to the uneven ground and the chance of getting hurt. He had to reach Kelly. And considering that the cops had loosened their cordon, he had to get there fast.

It was hard to wait, but Kelly didn't want to move before the guy had come fully into the room. His gaze would be focused on the bed, where she'd stuffed pillows under the covers. He wouldn't be expecting her to be hiding behind the door.

But he was so quiet she had to hold her breath for fear that he might hear her. Only the rustling of the trees outside, the occasional scrape of a limb across the roof, could possibly mask any sound she made, and she couldn't count on it, not when it was intermittent.

The door opened very slowly. More caution. It seemed to inch its way, as if he were prepared to stop moving if it made the least creak.

Holding the hammer high, she waited, schooling herself to a patience she had never thought she had, even as the rack of tension wound her nerves tighter and tighter until action seemed the only escape available.

As soon as he was inside. Wait. Just as soon as he was fully inside the room.

One step and she'd be able to swing. Just one step would bring her to him. The room was so dark she couldn't tell if he held any kind of a weapon. She squinted, trying to see his hands, unable to make out anything.

He finally crept past the partly open door. One more step, she told herself. Just one. The smell of his cologne reached her and she nearly gagged.

He hesitated and she held her breath, willing even her racing heart to settle down. It seemed so loud in her own ears now, she was sure he would hear it.

But he didn't turn her way. He just waited. Seconds stretched to a minute. Then, finally, another step into the room.

She took her step, hammer high.

Then, to her shock, she swung quickly and he spun, grabbing her arm in a viselike grip.

Hank was sure he could have made better time in a three-legged race. The sensation did not amuse him, even though he knew it was born of his desperation to get to Kelly.

Her plan had worked. By returning to her home, she had convinced the guy that everyone thought it was just a break-in, so he was willing to try again tonight. And Hank wasn't the least bit happy about it.

Every damaged muscle, bone and tendon in his body shrieked with agony, but he ignored the pain, focused on one goal only. He had to get to Kelly before that guy hurt her.

He'd have walked naked into the middle of a raging forest fire at that moment, just to get to Kelly. The protests of his body were paltry by comparison.

One house. Two houses. One more to go. God, he hoped she hadn't locked the doors.

His hip tried to collapse. Somehow, through sheer force of will, he overrode the weakness. Where the hell were the cops? They'd arrived faster last night.

Just a few more steps to her porch. Just a few more…

With her arm caught, the hammer was useless. Almost before she could try to fight loose, a fist punched her in the stomach. She lost her breath as pain blossomed, and she felt her knees giving way.

No! No! Fighting back pain, trying desperately to catch her breath, the world spinning, she felt another blow, a chop to the shoulder of the arm that held the hammer.

Her nerves went instantly numb. With something close to desperation and despair, she heard the hammer fall to the floor with a thud.

A moment later, he had spun her around, locking his arm around her neck, tightening it until it hurt.

At last she sucked in a breath of air, a painful breath. Adrenaline kicked even higher, forcing the cobwebs of shock and despair from her brain.

A cold thought snaked into her head. No matter what the outcome, she wasn't going to make this easy for him.

Some remembered words from her self-defense class

surfaced. She staggered a little, as if she were completely unsteady, trying to find out where his feet were.

Much to her relief, even though he tightened his arm around her throat, she felt one of his feet.

Then he punched her in the side of the head. For an instant the world flashed bright, and her ears started ringing. Everything seemed to go off-kilter.

Foot. Remember the foot.

Gathering everything she had left, she picked up her leg and brought her heel down on the top of his foot. Then, just a moment later, she collapsed, hanging her whole weight from his arm.

The combination was too much for him. He released her with a sharp groan, and she tumbled to the floor.

Dizzy, with an unending bell seeming to clang in her head, she rolled and felt for the damn hammer. She had to find it. Had to.

Except her fingers found nothing except a wooden floor.

And now her attacker was angry. Without warning, he kicked her. Maybe he missed his mark because a little higher and he would have done a lot of damage. Instead, he caught her right in the hip.

Pain shot through her like a fountain of fire, but she ignored it other than crying out. If he kicked her head next…

The thought added to her desperation. She crab-crawled away from his feet, arms out, seeking that hammer.

A foot landed on one of her hands, and she couldn't smother a scream as bones ground together.

Anger rose to join the fury of fear and she managed to roll, just a bit, just enough. She could see his shadow, and the instant she could, she pinwheeled her hips, took aim and kicked with all her remaining might at his knee.

He staggered, a shocked cry of pain escaping him. The pressure on her hand vanished.

She didn't even try to figure out if she could still move her fingers. She still had another hand, and dammit there was a hammer nearby. And while he tried to steady himself, she crawled as best she could, feeling for it.

For the first time in her life, she was absolutely certain that she was about to commit murder.

Hank heard the thuds, heard the cries as he barreled through the back door. Where the hell were the cops? Not caring if he was seen, considering what it sounded like was happening, he flicked on lights as he went, grabbed a two-by-four about two feet long from the living room floor as he passed through, and headed to Kelly's bedroom.

The door was open and he could see Kelly on the floor, her assailant towering over her. Running as fast as he could with that damn limp, he picked up speed somehow when he saw the guy was about to kick her.

He burst into the room, causing a moment of distraction. The assailant looked at him, an expression of shock on his face.

And Kelly, far from being down and out, took that moment to swing the hammer at the guy's leg.

And then, reprising the night before, but in much better form, Hank tackled him.

They hit the floor together, Hank's arms around his knees. He hung on tight, not wanting to give the guy a chance to get up.

"Run, Kelly. Get out of here."

But she apparently had other ideas.

Hank watched with horror the way she staggered as she reached her feet, the way she shook her head as if confused while he hung on to the wildly struggling assailant. But there was one thing she wasn't at all confused about.

She took a couple of unsteady steps, then seemed to gather

strength. And the next thing Hank knew, she was sitting on the guy's back and pummeling him with all her strength, as if she wouldn't be happy until he looked like pudding.

And finally, finally, a familiar voice called, "Sheriff! Drop your weapons!"

Thank God, Hank thought. Thank God.

Chapter 13

Three patients, one of whom was cuffed to a bed, hardly seemed like enough to make even Community Hospital's relatively small emergency room seem busy, so maybe it was all the deputies hovering around.

One side of Kelly's face was severely swollen from where she'd been kicked, and a black eye started to appear. Her hand was x-rayed with a portable unit, but nothing was broken. It was, however, rapidly approaching the size of a grapefruit. Her hip, too, was bruised, but otherwise fine.

She waited for the skull x-rays that had been ordered, but she was getting impatient to know if the sheriff had learned anything from the guy who attacked her.

And Hank was just plain impatient. He kept saying that he was fine, that all he'd done was tackle the guy, but they insisted on checking him out anyway. Finally, he managed to get them to open the curtain between his and Kelly's cubicles so he could lean over, look at her and say, "How are you doing, darlin'?"

She thrilled to the endearment, but was quite certain it had been tossed off casually. "I think I know how a prize-fighter feels after a few rounds in the ring, but I'm fine. I'm perfectly fine. I'm not even dizzy anymore."

"I swear, there were ten minutes there that felt like ten years."

"It was only five," she assured him, smiling with the uninjured side of her face. "Only five. But it did seem like ten."

"How do you know it was only five?"

"From the time I hit my beeper until Gage arrived, five minutes. They told me."

"Too damn long," he muttered grumpily.

"I heard that," Gage said, rounding the corner. "Sorry, still can't teleport, although I've been working on it. Things like roads and trees must be observed. And the foot patrols I had circling got there about the same time."

"You got there in plenty of time," Kelly assured him. "I didn't hit the beeper until he was in the bedroom."

The two men stared at her aghast.

Finally, Hank asked, "Why in the hell not?"

"Because I didn't want him to get away again."

Hank used a few choice cusswords that caused a nurse outside to call, "Not fit for a lady's ears, Hank Jackson. Cut it out."

Kelly had more important concerns. She looked at Gage. "Did he say my husband hired him?"

"Ask him yourself." With that Gage pushed back the curtain. Her attacker lay cuffed to the bed, his leg in a brace. When the curtain opened, so did his eyes, and he saw her. Surprise filled his face.

"So," she said, "did my husband hire you to kill me?"

"Lady, I ain't ever…"

"Shut up," she said calmly. "I'd recognize you anywhere. You attacked me in my parking garage and tried to drown me in a canal back home. Now you attacked me again."

"Two counts," Gage intoned. "Attempted murder. That's a long sentence."

But Kelly had seen the change in the man's face when he realized she could identify him as her attacker from Miami. He no longer looked quite so stony-faced. And the stoniness lessened with Gage's pronouncement.

"Yeah," the guy said finally. "Your husband hired me."

It was all she needed to hear. Exactly what she needed the cops to hear. Now, at last, it was over.

Not only was her stalker in custody, but very soon Dean would be as well.

As the final fear lifted from her shoulders, she felt as if she could float.

"You know what this looks like?" Hank asked as he helped Kelly up the steps to his house hours later.

"What?"

"The halt leading the lame, or something. Both of us can barely walk right now."

"You must be sore."

"Darlin', I couldn't possibly be any sorer than you."

There was that word again. Despite every mental warning to herself that it was just casual, it warmed her anyway. It felt like a hug, and tickled her deep inside.

Hank led her to the living room sofa and dug out one of the ice packs the hospital had given them. He crunched it to activate it, then gently pressed it to her swollen face.

"Every time I look at you," he said, "I want to smash that guy's face in. And I'm not inclined to violence by nature."

"I'm fine," she said, daring to reach out and take his free

hand. "For a minute there I wanted to kill him, too. But I'm glad I didn't because now we'll get Dean."

"I agree." He gave her a crooked smile. "That makes me feel somewhat better." He squeezed her hand. "It's too bad you're so banged up."

"Yeah, but it'll pass. I'm still alive."

"Thank God for that. But no, I'm being very selfish."

"Selfish how?"

His smile grew even more crooked. "I just want to take you to bed and make love to you until we're so exhausted we can't move. But right now…" He shook his head.

She caught her breath and turned toward him, nudging the ice pack aside. "I'd like that. I'd really like that."

"But not yet," he said firmly. "Cripes, it'd be a circus between the two of us. You have a huge bruise on your hip, your neck is sore, your head's a mess… Nope."

She sighed and closed her eyes briefly. "You're right. I hate it that you're right."

"Me, too, darlin'."

Her eyes popped open. Well, one of them did. The other managed to become a slit through which she could barely see.

"Don't call me that," she said. It hurt too much, knowing he couldn't possibly mean it. "Don't call me that unless you mean it." Then she closed her eyes again, amazed that she'd been bold enough to say that. Well, having nearly died— again—seemed to have made certain niceties a waste of time. But her heart stuttered as she waited to hear…nothing. He would say nothing because he was too nice to admit that he didn't mean it, and he couldn't possibly mean it.

The silence seemed endless. Her heart ached with loss. How could she have been such a fool to fall in love again. And after only a handful of days?

Finally, unable to stand the tension and silence, she opened her eyes again and looked at him.

He stared at her, looking as if his heart, his soul, felt suspended by a thread. Well, that settled it, she thought. If her simple words could strike terror in him he wanted little to do with her. Maybe she should start packing right now.

But then his husky voice froze her in place.

"I mean it," he said finally. "I've never called anyone that before. But…you don't want me to mean it."

Her heart stopped. Her breathing nearly stopped. She sounded like a frog when she finally forced words out. "I don't? Why the heck not?"

To her amazement, he was the one who seemed to hold his breath now. Then, "But…you're going back to Miami, right? Now that the guy is caught?"

"I'm going back to Miami for a court date and maybe later to testify at a trial. Whether I stay there…well, that's not my decision alone."

"Are you thinking about coming back here?"

She just looked at him.

Finally, she saw frustration stamp his face. Her heart dared to lift a tiny bit. "Kelly, I'm just a cowboy. I don't know how to play games. If there's something you need me to say, tell me what the hell it is. Please."

She felt a twinge. He thought she was trying to play games? Maybe she was. Maybe it was just time to settle this. She had almost died again last night. How could she possibly be afraid of being the first one to step off this ledge? Whether or not she took the first step, it was going to hurt like hell if he didn't want her. It wasn't as if she could avoid the pain by not speaking. "I want to know if you want me to stay here. I want to know if I might have a home here."

He said nothing for so long that her heart quivered and her

stomach began to drop. This was it. He was seeking a kind way to tell her to forget it.

But when he started to speak at last, it took a second for his words to penetrate the growing fog of her despair. "I want you to stay. I need you to stay. I realize that we don't really know each other yet, but… well…I'm pretty damn sure I'm in love with you."

A joyous shock rolled through her, leaving her almost light-headed, banishing her aches and pains, and she smiled—amazing considering how swollen half of her face was. "Really?"

"Really." And once again he was holding his breath, apparently as much on tenterhooks as she had just been.

"I love you, too," she said finally, leaning painfully toward him to brush just the lightest of kisses against his lips. "I'm sure of it. I love you. And I want to stay with you."

"In this one-horse town?"

"The one-horse town is beautiful with you in it."

He studied her face, seeking the truth in it, and finally he threw back his head and let out a loud, "Yeehaw!"

Well, he was a cowboy after all, and his lady had just filled his heart with joy. And then she giggled and squeezed his hand.

"I love you," he said again, gingerly wrapping his arm around her. "I love you. Now hurry up and get well so I can show you how much."

She snuggled into his arms, as if she had been made just for him. Because suddenly and with certainty, she was sure of it. The joy was almost more than she could bear. "Count on it, cowboy. Count on it."

* * * * *

Harlequin

ROMANTIC
SUSPENSE

COMING NEXT MONTH

Available July 26, 2011

#1667 DOUBLE DECEPTION
Code Name: Danger
Merline Lovelace

#1668 SPECIAL OPS BODYGUARD
The Kelley Legacy
Beth Cornelison

#1669 COLD CASE REUNION
Native Country
Kimberly Van Meter

#1670 BEST MAN FOR THE JOB
Meredith Fletcher

You can find more information on upcoming
Harlequin® titles, free excerpts and more at
www.HarlequinInsideRomance.com.

REQUEST YOUR FREE BOOKS!
2 FREE NOVELS PLUS 2 FREE GIFTS!

❦ Harlequin®

ROMANTIC
SUSPENSE

Sparked by Danger, Fueled by Passion.

YES! Please send me 2 FREE Harlequin® Romantic Suspense novels and my 2 FREE gifts (gifts are worth about $10). After receiving them, if I don't wish to receive any more books, I can return the shipping statement marked "cancel." If I don't cancel, I will receive 4 brand-new novels every month and be billed just $4.49 per book in the U.S. or $5.24 per book in Canada. That's a saving of at least 14% off the cover price! It's quite a bargain! Shipping and handling is just 50¢ per book in the U.S. and 75¢ per book in Canada.* I understand that accepting the 2 free books and gifts places me under no obligation to buy anything. I can always return a shipment and cancel at any time. Even if I never buy another book, the two free books and gifts are mine to keep forever.

240/340 HDN FEFR

Name _____ (PLEASE PRINT) _____

Address _____ Apt. #

City _____ State/Prov. _____ Zip/Postal Code

Signature (if under 18, a parent or guardian must sign)

Mail to the **Reader Service:**

IN U.S.A.: P.O. Box 1867, Buffalo, NY 14240-1867
IN CANADA: P.O. Box 609, Fort Erie, Ontario L2A 5X3

Not valid for current subscribers to Harlequin Romantic Suspense books.

Want to try two free books from another line?
Call 1-800-873-8635 or visit www.ReaderService.com.

* Terms and prices subject to change without notice. Prices do not include applicable taxes. Sales tax applicable in N.Y. Canadian residents will be charged applicable taxes. Offer not valid in Quebec. This offer is limited to one order per household. All orders subject to credit approval. Credit or debit balances in a customer's account(s) may be offset by any other outstanding balance owed by or to the customer. Please allow 4 to 6 weeks for delivery. Offer available while quantities last.

Your Privacy—The Reader Service is committed to protecting your privacy. Our Privacy Policy is available online at www.ReaderService.com or upon request from the Reader Service.

We make a portion of our mailing list available to reputable third parties that offer products we believe may interest you. If you prefer that we not exchange your name with third parties, or if you wish to clarify or modify your communication preferences, please visit us at www.ReaderService.com/consumerschoice or write to us at Reader Service Preference Service, P.O. Box 9062, Buffalo, NY 14269. Include your complete name and address.

HRS11B

Once bitten, twice shy. That's Gabby Wade's motto—
especially when it comes to Adamson men.
And the moment she meets Jon Adamson her theory
is confirmed. But with each encounter a little something
sparks between them, making her wonder if she's been
too hasty to dismiss this one!

Enjoy this sneak peek from ONE GOOD REASON
by Sarah Mayberry, available August 2011
from Harlequin® Superromance®.

Gabby Wade's heartbeat thumped in her ears as she marched to her office. She wanted to pretend it was because of her brisk pace returning from the file room, but she wasn't that good a liar.

Her heart was beating like a tom-tom because Jon Adamson had touched her. In a very male, very possessive way. She could still feel the heat of his big hand burning through the seat of her khakis as he'd steadied her on the ladder.

It had taken every ounce of self-control to tell him to unhand her. What she'd really wanted was to grab him by his shirt and, well, explore all those urges his touch had instantly brought to life.

While she might not like him, she was wise enough to understand that it wasn't always about liking the other person. Sometimes it was about pure animal attraction.

Refusing to think about it, she turned to work. When she'd typed in the wrong figures three times, Gabby admitted she was too tired and too distracted. Time to call it a day.

As she was leaving, she spied Jon at his workbench in the shop. His head was propped on his hand as he studied blueprints. It wasn't until she got closer that she saw his eyes were shut.

He looked oddly boyish. There was something innocent and unguarded in his expression. She felt a weakening in her resistance to him.

"Jon." She put her hand on his shoulder, intending to shake him awake. Instead, it rested there like a caress.

His eyes snapped open.

"You were asleep."

"No, I was, uh, visualizing something on this design." He gestured to the blueprint in front of him then rubbed his eyes.

That gesture dealt a bigger blow to her resistance. She realized it wasn't only animal attraction pulling them together. She took a step backward as if to get away from the knowledge.

She cleared her throat. "I'm heading off now."

He gave her a smile, and she could see his exhaustion.

"Yeah, I should, too." He stood and stretched. The hem of his T-shirt rose as he arched his back and she caught a flash of hard male belly. She looked away, but it was too late. Her mind had committed the image to permanent memory.

And suddenly she knew, for good or bad, she'd never look at Jon the same way again.

Find out what happens next in ONE GOOD REASON, available August 2011 from Harlequin® Superromance®!

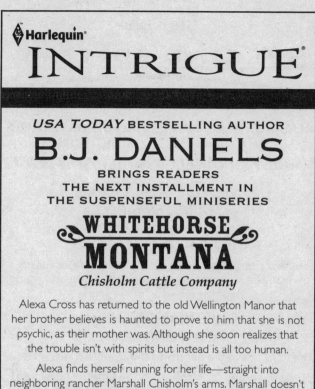